The Reluctant Rapist

By the same author

How Do You Do (a play)
Five Plays
New Plays from the Black Theatre (editor)
The Duplex: A Black Love Fable in Four Movements
The Hungered One: Early Writings
Four Dynamite Plays
The Theme Is Blackness: The Corner and Other Plays

The Reluctant Rapist

ED BULLINS

HARPER & ROW, PUBLISHERS

New York, Evanston, San Francisco, London

FIRST EDITION

Designed by Patricia Dunbar

Library of Congress Cataloging in Publication Data

Bullins, Ed.
    The reluctant rapist.

    I. Title
PZ4.B9357Re   [PS3552.U45]   813'.5'4   73–4143
ISBN 0–06–010579–8

To my Father . . . who also had a street jones

Street
Jones

I got a street jones
baby
run 'til the wheels
roll off

I got a street fever
lil' mamma
turnin' corners
cause I'm
fly

My habit's runnin'
honey
so you know
not to have
an attitude

I'm a corner boy
sister
so you know
where I'm
comin' from

I'm a street nigger
girl
so any
tears for
me don't

lose too
soon

It's a cold shot
sweetmeat
but I've
known your
mamma
a long time
before I've
known
you.

lyrics: Ed Bullins
music: Pat Patrick
Downpat Music Co. (BMI)

Evening lay in Figueroa Street with the sky purpling overhead. Ernest and I walked along saying little and watching the cars and the street. We passed a tuxedo shop, the lights in the back off, and a dummy in the display window wore an After Five jacket that I couldn't afford. We turned at the corner into a liquor store. Coolness waited inside, the room well lighted. Two men stood behind the counter, one white with a large bald head and a negro who looked like a postal clerk.

"What ta ya drink, man?" Ernest asked.

"Wine."

The store was filled with customers. Little black spindly-legged kids getting sodas and Kool-Aid. Older girls waiting in line for cigarettes, holding Cokes and popping gum in their wide mouths.

"C'mon; step on up," the bald man said.

The other man acted as cashier unless there was a bill larger than a five to cash. The large-headed man stood beside the cash register and looked over the other's shoulder.

"That's five, sixteen and twenty-six for the cigarettes, and that makes forty-sev'van, sister." He spoke as he counted up each customer's items.

The men's voices mingled.

"Okay, step right up here, girlie," the bald one would say.

"Yeah, whatcha got?" the other man asked.

And then there would be the: "Dolla forty-one fo dat beer, ten fo da paper and . . ."

Ernest pulled out a half gallon of vin rosé from the cooler.

1

"Is this awlright?"

"Yeah, it's great with me."

"Can you stand some beer, man?" he wanted to know.

"Yeah, get a six-pack."

There were two girls between us and the next customer. One had on tight pink capris and her rear decollated toward us. The other girl had on black pants that had the foot stirrups that made the trousers outline her hips and thighs. Both wore deep-cut thin jerseys.

"Ooweee," the one in pink pants said. "Chile, if I don't ketch me a trick tonight, I sho will be in a mess with mah ole man."

"I wish you luck, honey," the other replied. "There's so much heat out here tonight I might wake up tomorrow with a sunburn."

"You safe, sweetie."

"I'm really not ready to give it a chance. Really!"

"Really?"

"Really, baby!"

The bald man closed the cash drawer and licked his lips.

"You're next," he said to the girls.

"Yeah, step on up," the dark man said.

The first girl put two packs of cigarettes on the counter.

"That's twenty-six and twenty-six. . . . Will there be anything else, girlie?" the white man said.

"Yeah, give me four cans of . . ."

The other clerk went in back when he found there were none of the girl's brand left out front.

"I've got a good deal I can give you on that brand, girlie," the man said. "A real barg'in."

"Yeah? How much, baby?" the girl in pink pants asked.

"Oh, I have to figure it out. Why don't you stop back about closin' time?"

"Is it a good deal, honey?" the other girl asked.

He continued smiling at the first girl.

"I'll think 'bout it. . . . Maybe I'll see you 'round two," the girl said.

"You can't do better, girlie," the big man said as the negro returned.

2

The girls switched out, their heels clacking out into the summer night. "Well, that will take some of the weight off," the girl in pink said. "If I can jest get me another trick before two I'll be straight with Sonny."

"Now whatcha boys want?" the bald man said.

"How fuckin' big do boys grow where you come from, mister?" Ernie asked.

"I only asked ya what you wanted, fellow," the bald man said. "Don't be so smart. If ya don't want what I got ya don't have ta buy."

The other clerk pulled the bottles and the beer toward him. He pushed them out of sight behind a display sign.

"You don't have to buy here if you don't want to," the negro said.

"Nobody's talkin' to you, man," Ernest said.

"But I'm talking to you."

"The man said he wasn't speaking to you," I said.

A crowd was forming, mostly kids with a few older people peering over their shoulders.

"If you boys are lookin' . . ."

"If you say boy once more, mahthafukker," Ernest said, "I'm goin' ta find out how much man you are."

The bald man pulled a snub-nosed .38 from under the counter. A few from the crowd ran out the door and there was murmuring and ducking behind us.

"You want ta try it, *boy,*" he said.

"I'm goin' ta call the police," the black man said, moving away from the counter and edging toward the back.

A man in gray denims stepped up and stood beside Ernest and me.

"I saw what happened, Saul," he said to the bald man. "You provoked these here boys."

The white man lowered the gun and pointed his finger at the new man's very dark face. "Wait a minute, Johnson!"

"Now, Johnson, this ain't none of your business," the negro clerk said, looking afraid to go in back now or to use the telephone on the counter.

Johnson didn't seem to hear them but turned to Ernest and me.

3

"Why don't you fellas go someplace else? This man's gonna put ya in trouble," he said, indicating the bald man with a nod.

With his free hand on the cash register and the other dropped below the counter clutching the pistol, the bald man stood as far away from the counter as possible. He and the negro almost huddled in the same spot.

"You better get rid of that there gun," the black man in denims told him.

The bald man removed his hand from the cash register and then showed his now empty hand. "Johnson, you been a customer of mine for over ten years, and if you had really seen what had gone on you wouldn't be stickin' your nose in here. These boys are probably gettin' ready to rob me. . . ."

"Mother fucker!" Ernest tried to get past Johnson but the man blocked him from touching the counter and I held his arms.

"Take yo finger out of my face!" Johnson said when the bald man lifted his hand to shield himself.

"Now, Johnson . . ." the negro clerk began.

"Shut up; you hear me talkin' to yo boss."

I pulled Ernest's sleeve and we both turned, silently, and walked out the door, pushing past the crowd in front. Ernest screamed one last remark over his shoulder: "You dirty Jew pussy sucker!"

From inside the store the last thing I heard was the owner asking Johnson why he could call us boys and the owner couldn't.

We headed down toward Vernon, Ernest cursing all the way and balling up his fist and pounding it into the center of his palm.

"Man, one of these days it's gonna be too bad, that's all," he said. "It's just gonna be too bad."

I agreed with him.

A Ralph's Market stands at the corner of Vernon and Figueroa, and on Sunday nights the crowds pack its aisles. We waited in line behind five people before our turn came, and the cashier asked me to show my I.D.

4

"So you were in the navy?" the cashier asked. She was an ocher shade and had her hair clipped in bangs across her eyes.

"Yeah, for four years."

"Ever been to Japan?"

"No, I was on the East Coast and in Europe."

"My husband's on a carrier," she said with the line growing behind us.

She packaged our wine and beer and set it in a shopping cart. I wished she were darker to remind me better of a girl I had known once whose husband had been in the navy and in Japan while we fell in and out of love one winter and spring.

"It's pretty good we went there," Ernest said when we got back outside. "We got a whole case of Amber & Brauer for two-cans-for-a-quarter and a gallon of pluck for a dollar forty-nine."

"Yeah, that's somethin' new on me."

"Are you gonna go back to see her?" Ernest asked.

"Nawh," I said.

"She was hittin' on ya, man, and she looks pretty tough."

"I don't think I'll go back."

Ernest told me that there was always room for one more girl as we strolled up the street. On a corner, opposite the liquor store, we met Rick standing.

"Well, if it ain't brother Ernest . . . and his friend, ha ha ha," he said.

He wore an aged suit, which seemed routine for him, but his shirt was fresh and a blue tie hung down his shirt front with a brassy clip attached. His scalp was freshly shaven and he smiled widely.

"Hey, Rick, how you doin'?" Ernest replied.

"Heard you two just upset the white man across the street."

"News really travels," Ernest said. "How did you find out?"

"Oh, I saw the crowd at the door and went to look but by that time a gun was in sight, so I thought I'd best come ov'va on this side of the street, seein' that the devil's eyes ain't too good."

"The who?" I asked.

"The devil, the white man," Rick said. "Don't you know that that Jew is the devil?"

"No, I didn't. Are you a Muslim?"

He didn't answer right away; he looked to Ernest.

"What's your friend's name?"

"His name's Steve."

"Well, then, Steve," he said, turning to me. "Just because I see the truth that the Honorable Elijah Muhammad, the true messenger of Allah, speaks doesn't make me anything more than an enlightened black man."

"I'm sorry," I said.

"Don't be sorry," he said. "In fact the majority of your brothers are walking these streets right now without the understanding that you have. I know you just want Freedom, Justice and Equality like all of our black brothers . . . or don't you, ha ha ha. I only use the language that I feel you're intelligent enough to grasp . . . you do understand what I'm saying? Language is my game; all words have a time and place somewhere. If I were a Muslim I wouldn't be ushering this program at the church of these dead black folks." He motioned to the open church doors behind him and glanced at his watch. A long aisle led downward to the pulpit and above the rostrum a banner spread out across organ pipes, spelling out the name of the Holiness African Baptist Chapel.

"What do you mean by dead black folks?" I asked.

"I mean that they are dead 'cause they don't know the truth about their black selves."

A group of people walked down the side street, approaching the corner where we stood.

"Here's some of the good brothers and sisters now," Ernest said, disgust sounding at the edges of his voice.

"Good evening, brothers. . . . Sister Price's lookin' good tonight. . . . How're yawhl?" Rick greeted the small band as they entered the doors.

"I see you have some more drinks," he said when turning back to us. "Well, I hope you two are able to keep your heads." He walked toward the doors.

"See you later, Rick," Ernest called out.

He turned back and caught us before we started away. "Who's at the house?"

"Connie Jones, Olu, Len and Lou and us," Ernest said.

"Tell everybody I'll be over after I get through here," Rick said.

After he had left and Ernest and I had neared the house we had to wait for the street light to change to GO before we could cross.

"Why didn't Rick give us a hand if he was at the store?"

"Oh, Rick," Ernest sighed. "He's more mouf den anything. You'll never see the good professor gettin' his toes mashed rushing ta a hassle."

"Where's he from?"

"Back east. Maryland, I think."

"Yeah?" I said. "What part?"

"I think Len knows," Ernest said.

When we got back to the house, rock-and-roll played on the radio and Lou was teaching Olu to twist. The African interpreted the dance as a form of his tribal music, but Lou wasn't happy with the results.

"No, no, no, no, no, no, *no!*" she told him. "Twist your hips, Olu, your hips. Please don't do that humpin' . . . it don' look so nice with me."

"You missed the African program," Len said to Ernest and me.

"We only went down the street."

"It was only on fifteen minutes," Lou hollered. "That goddamned Lenard had us listen to that ole-timey shit for over an hour before some whiteman came on actin' like he knew all 'bout Africa."

"Yes, it was pretty bad." Len shook his head in disgust.

"C'mon, twist, Olu," Lou said. "Like this. Twist, like this. Twist!"

"If you're going to have a program about Africa," Len continued, lecturing in his precise voice, "or even negroes, then let an African or some brother get on up and speak for himself."

"Mahthafukker," Ernest said. It seemed the appropriate thing for him to say then.

"Twist, twist, twist," Lou cried. "Twist!"

Connie was in the kitchen stirring a pot on the stove. I told Len we had seen Rick and that he would be over when he completed his ushering job.

"Oh, that shit again," Len said. "He's still trying to con those church people into giving him a scholarship."

"So that's it," Ernest said.

"Yeah, and the beauty of it is that he'll get it." Len spoke with admiration.

"Where's he from?"

"Rick? He's from Maryland . . . Eastern Shore Maryland."

And then I understood the whining accent which recalled forgotten voices. I thought of the times I had spent in Eastern Shore Maryland. Of the hot summer weeks and the bleak winter. Of how long it had been and the differences. . . . The differences were in almost everything. Even my name was different then. Down home they called me Dandy.

"We're makin' a regular country boy outta you, Dandy Benson," Aunt Bessie said, wiping the flour from her hands.

Dandy laughed behind her back as she stooped to shove the biscuits in the oven, and muttered "Like hell" under his breath.

"What did you say?" she asked.

"Nothin'."

Dandy took his swatter and eased over in back of Marie Ann to smash the fly she was stalking.

"Git on away from here, Dandy Benson," she giggled. Her brown face burst into joy.

"This is man's work, Marie Ann," Dandy drawled.

She pulled at his wrist and they began wrestling across the floor on the far side of the great kitchen from Aunt Bessie. Marie Ann's large muscular legs strained below her shorts as the two pushed and jerked. Dandy held her tight, on the sneak, to feel her young breasts.

8

"You kids, you kids break that up," Aunt Bessie yelled. "Break that up, you hear me, Dandy and Marie?"

They parted with Marie getting the last tap with her swatter on Dandy's rear.

"Dandy, I want you to stay away from Marie," Aunt Bessie said for at least the hundredth time, Dandy thought. "You two are together too much and if anything happens to that girl, Dandy Benson, I'm going to see that somebody goes to jail and that goes for you too."

Dandy and Marie had heard Aunt Bessie's threats before; they had heard them as a regular part of their long summer days together; their being caught in childish play each day was almost routine, or the near miss of being discovered kissing or hugging, and then the following mock violence of the confrontation by the old lady they both loved. Even if they had been guilty, if Dandy had been so fortunate as to be fully worthy of her suspicions and the woman had carried out her promises, they both knew that they would continue loving Aunt Bessie, as nearly everyone did.

Aunt Bessie claimed love as her own, and in this manner she took the children of the poor and wretched and overworked into her warmth. She took those who would love her most.

Dandy looked out one of the windows surrounding the kitchen and wished that he had opportunity to test Aunt Bessie's threats.

Times were better now, he thought. There was so much more for him to like his second summer in Mary's Shore, Maryland. He liked the way the tan and brown of the sand and mud roads wound through the dried weed fields and meadows more this summer than his first lonely year, and he liked the animals: the dozen ducks, the eight pigs, the horse, Jim, and the couple hundred chickens that Aunt Bess and Uncle Clyde kept on their sixteen-acre farm. He even kind of liked Uncle Clyde, a little bit at least, and surely the second summer's entire bunch better than the ones of his first vacation in Maryland. Even the year before that first one in Eastern Shore, spent in New Jersey with his near-white Aunt Martha, there wasn't the same dismal emptiness as the vacation of the first year with Aunt

Bessie, even though there was no one in New Jersey with him but Aunt Martha and her maid, cook and handyman, who doubled at driving the shiny new black Buick and was called "the chauffeur."

The first summer with Aunt Bessie, the kids had been either too young or all from the same little town of Chester, Pennsylvania, except him, and Dandy couldn't stomach much of their attempting to convert the freedom of Aunt Bess's farm into an extension of little Chester.

But this year there was Roy Howes, and there were Jack, Marie Ann and Richard Bowen. And there was Ida.

Aunt Bessie boarded out kids for the state adoption, correction and welfare agencies, and in the summer she and Uncle Clyde took in additional summer guests from the city. Dandy was from Philadelphia—that's why they had begun calling him Dandy, from the jitter-bug clothes he arrived in and his cool impractical walk, which was difficult to show on the soft dirt roads in his snake-skin, pointy-)ed shoes which he had to abandon for loafers; but he still hadn't altogether dropped the strut because he *knew* the city had made him to be different from the other boys there in that farmland.

"Go out and empty the garbage, Dandy," Aunt Bessie said. "Uncle Clyde and Jack and the little boys will be home soon."

That was a job that Dandy did well. He enjoyed the pull the bucket gave his muscles when he lifted the tin container and carried the swishing mess outside and across the yard to the pig barrel. The two dogs, a young German shepherd named Pudgy, and a collie, Cisco, always followed him across the yard begging him to drop them a scrap or throw them crusts as he sometimes did.

A wooden cover was on the barrel and Dandy had to slide it off with one hand while holding the bucket high so the dogs would not poke their snouts in and drag garbage around the yard and later get sick, their heaved up stomach contents drawing flies. Whenever Aunt Bessie cleaned chickens she especially warned Dandy, for one day Pudgy poked his head in the slop bucket quickly and pulled out a long chicken gut tied together with other chicken guts, and the shepherd and Cisco had dragged the garbage about the yard while several chickens, who had slipped under their fence and constantly ran the yard, chased after the scraps the dogs dropped and tore off. The hens pecked furiously away at the raw meat as if they didn't know they were devouring their brothers, and Aunt Bessie had gotten ill.

So with care Dandy lifted the bucket and sluiced the contents into the mixture. He stood and watched as the large pieces floated to the top and then were sucked under in the crawling stew, while air bubbles burped and the mess stirred internally and gave off yeasty sounds and sourer smells. The dogs' whines did not even muffle the popping of the pigs' pudding.

Dandy stood just off the driveway, which half-mooned around the house and cut the yard in two, pushing the workrooms, barn and henhouse into the background. The slop barrel hunkered beside an old wooden truck trailer that had been mounted on cinder blocks to the right of the house. Uncle Clyde used the trailer for a tool room and stored his pig and chicken feed in its cool wooden gloom.

The horse compound, stall, barn and henhouse with a shabby assortment of several other buildings formed a broken-toothed back wall to the yard. In front of the henhouse was a tree with a swing hanging from its lower branches. Dandy remembered the first summer when there had been two little dark girls with the whitest of whites in their eyes to swing on the now empty swing. He turned and put the top back upon the barrel. At the rear of the barn, henhouse and buildings was the manure pile, and down a small hill to ground, spongy wet in the autumn rains, was the pigpen with four large pigs in one half of the compound and four little porkers on the other side. Dandy would feed them after supper when it began to get dark and cool.

Behind the pigpen were woods for a quarter of a mile and behind the trees were the church campgrounds; every year in August the Mary's Shore colored community gave an ole-timey camp meetin'. Mary's Shore was in fact a town two miles away, two country miles, and where Aunt Bessie's farm sat was closer to the crossing of Mt. Holy. Three roads converged like blinded snakes: the road from

11

Hamilton, the twisted and adventurous route from Bicksley, and the Biltmore dust highway. On one corner was a store with an ancient filling pump, an old-style one with gauges in the head and the liquid moving down the glass bulb like bubbling sand in an hourglass. On the other corner was Sister Ossie Mae Hewett's house and land. And at the apex of the triangle was the Mt. Holy Methodist Church. Opposite Aunt Bessie's field, running a quarter mile toward the crossing, was the Mt. Holy Cemetery. The small settlement of black farmers and laborers called themselves "M" Holy more than anything else.

"You sho drag feet, Dandy Wandy," Marie Ann said when he entered the kitchen. She tickled the back of his head with the fly swatter as he went past. Aunt Bessie was again bent over the oven. She was a large-boned, heavy-fleshed woman who eternally laughed and joked, showing her flashy store teeth. She was very proud of her teeth, almost as proud of them as she was of herself. Dandy thought that the way she managed things and worked the love and affection from people was how he'd seen others do. Up north, on Saturdays, Dandy ran errands for the girls in the neighborhood whorehouse. He had seen how the madam had managed the girls, and he had seen and heard how the pimps, sliding up to the curb in their long shiny cars that the ghetto kids called "hawgs" had always messed with the minds of the whores. And in Dandy's mind, Aunt Bess was one of these people. She was shrewd and open, with a heart big enough to satisfy even herself. But Dandy knew her, knew she believed in nothing, as he did, not even in the God she went in search of three times a week at the whitewashed church up the road, for she was what Dandy called a phony, though she was nice, one of his favorite people of all those he knew, so he liked her very much while not trusting her a bit.

"Why, here they come," Aunt Bessie exclaimed in her booming voice. "Here come my boys."

An old Packard groaned around the driveway and halted. The front passenger door opened and a tall dark young man stepped out and turned away from the house and headed for the outhouse. From the rear doors skipped a brown laughing boy and a thin dark one circled the car to join the other.

"Hey, hey, Fatso," the brown boy screamed in mirth as the dogs pranced and yapped about him.

"Ahhh, Roy, you better not tell," the darker one said. "Ahhh . . . Roy."

"Heee hee heee . . . Oooooo, man." The brown boy laughed and began running around the car with the dark one after him, the dogs completing the circle.

"Git on in the house and get ready fo dinner," the man in the car said. He sat in his driver's place and shouted through the window.

The two boys came in the house, letting the screen door bang behind them.

"You little boys stop lettin' that screen door bang," Marie Ann shouted.

"Oh, shut up, girl," one of them said.

"Wait, wait. . . . Before you two little boys get ready for supper I want you to walk up to Sister Ossie Mae Hewett's where Ida is workin'," Aunt Bessie said.

"Yes, Aunt Bessie," the dark boy said.

"Walk home with Ida and Sister Ossie's goin' ta send back some tomatoes and peaches."

"Hee . . . hee . . ." Roy chortled.

"Didn't you hear Aunt Bess, boy?" Marie Ann asked. "What's wrong with you little boys?"

"But, Aunt Bess . . . hee hee." Roy tried to choke out more, but his laugh bent him over near to the floor.

"Look at that silly boy," Aunt Bessie said, her face cracking into a smile for the joke that had to come.

"What's wrong with that boy?" Marie Ann wanted to know.

"Don't listen to him, Aunt Bessie," the dark boy said. "He's tryin' ta make fun ah me. Don't listen ta him, Aunt Bess."

"Aunt Bess, Fatso . . . he . . . he," Roy began, pointing at the thin boy, "he tried . . . heee hee heeee."

13

"I don't want to hear about Richard Bowen," Aunt Bessie blustered when Roy stretched out on the floor and sobbed with mirth. "Get on up to Sister Ossie Mae's and get Ida."

The boys left finally, with Richard grabbing a slim stick from the woodshed in back of the trailer and crying "Oooo, man" and chasing Roy around the drive and out in front of the house and up the road with the old man's shouts from the car all the while warning that they better get about their little businesses.

Dandy was helping Marie Ann set the table when the tall youth came in and slammed the screen door.

"There's mah big son," Aunt Bess said and shuddered when the door flew shut. "How did it go today, son?"

"Awlright, Aunt Bessie," he said, deepening his voice on purpose to a musical baritone.

"How's my big bro Bowen," Marie Ann said, pushing herself against the youth to make him lean sideways.

"Whatcha doin' dere, *Maurey?*" The boy slipped into a playful drawl and began pushing her across the floor.

"Bo, stop pushin' your little sister," Marie Ann giggled. She tried to tickle him as they jostled their way across the room.

"Dandy, come and pull this here girl offa me," Jack Bowen called.

"No, Dandy, don't you dare, Dandy," Marie screamed, laughing as she acted like she was about to be raped. "Help me, please help me, Dandy," she pleaded.

"I'm neutral," Dandy called out, watching their mock battle, seeing the sinews bulge in Marie Anne's legs and her solid behind below the narrow waist fight the material of the shorts.

"Dandy, you better help out one of them or ole Aunt Bessie's gonna jump in to even it up," the old woman teased and began rolling up imaginary sleeves and wetting thumbs on tongue as she threw up her dukes.

Dandy ran to the sink and pulled a damp towel from the rack and twirled it tight three times and ran across to the squirming couple and popped the towel on the seat of Marie Ann's shorts.

"Ohh . . . Dandy, you dirty dog," she whimpered.

14

And he popped her again, a loud and cracking whack.

"That's for the fly swatter, Marie," he said.

"Hey, what you kids doin' in dere?" the man in the car called in.

"See here, your Uncle Clyde is goin' to get you," Aunt Bess said and moved over to the door, blocking the man's view.

"Jack Bowen, you go and clean up," she said.

The couple parted.

"Just don't worry so much about inside of here when you ain't in, Clyde," Aunt Bessie hollered. "Just don't stick your nose in so much," she said to the old man in the old Packard.

"I'll be stickin' mah foot somewhere if'in I don't git some peace around here," the man in the car said.

When Jack let Marie loose, Dandy spun around with the girl swinging at him. When they were inside the front room he let her catch him and she slapped at his grinning face until they began kissing. Aunt Bessie called her to finish setting the table.

Dandy didn't want to go back into the kitchen with his just having gotten kissed and then suddenly having to act like nothing had happened. He didn't know if he could be normal.

That time at Doris's he hadn't been normal, and he had really tried that time. No matter how he tried it always betrayed him. In fact, he knew it was *he* who betrayed himself.

He had met Doris at school. She was in his homeroom class and Doris had been pretty hard to miss. She was the oldest of either girls or boys for having been put away in reform school for almost three years and she was also the largest and loudest.

Doris was evil to his way of thinking . . . a type of evil which fascinated him. Not only did she curse like she wanted, she did everything else she wanted. She threatened the boys in class as well as the girls, but it was especially the boys she had made fear her, and she didn't just bluff. Of course there was probably bluster in her statements to the boys that she could cut or pull their "things" off if they messed with her or got in her way but most believed her, for she had been known to scratch girls up and hit the boys so hard on

15

their arms and in the chest that they swore she hit like a man. Most fourteen-year-olds have not been struck by a man's full punch, but Doris's rep was secure.

Somehow she never bothered Dandy before they became friends. For all of Dandy's swagger, essentially he was a quiet boy. After school he would go home and work on his motorbike, or if he couldn't find any defect in it, he and his friend Homer would take a ride or go by some girl's house. Homer lived next door to him and they were the only two in their neighborhood who had motorbikes. Dandy had gotten his by begging his mother for two long weeks. Homer had gotten his six weeks later by taking an extra job after school. Some days Dandy didn't ride with Homer or tamper with his bike's efficiency. He went around the corner to the Eighth Street gym in the basement of the police station. There he trained for the future. That's what he thought he would be someday, a fighter.

Columbia Avenue in North Philly in some of its neon stretches has a bar at every corner and one, two or three in between. It is a street of pawnshops, trolley cars, pimps, markets, jazz, real estate offices, hustlers, the hustled, lawyers, whores, junkies, blues and more blues, movies . . . and bars—the main artery of a ghetto, Dandy's neighborhood.

Up north, in the city, Dandy was mostly called Stevie. And the Saturday afternoon that Stevie Benson and Homer met Snoopy and his boys, the "Avenue" was jumpin', a drunk's delight and a cock hound's carnival. Stevie and Homer had crossed Broad and passed the five-and-ten when they were stopped by the five boys who stepped from the alley next to the show.

"Hey, what's happenin', man?" the dark wiry leader said to Stevie.

"How's it goin', Homer?" one of the boys said to Stevie's friend.

"What the fuck is this supposed to be, man?" Homer asked. Homer was older than any of them and the boys in front of him grinned and backed off. Stevie didn't know any of the gang.

"I said what's happenin'," the leader spoke again.

"Nothin'. What's happen'n' with you, man?" Stevie replied.

16

No one else spoke. Homer strolled to the curb and sat on the bumper of a car. The other boys faded aside, leaving the pair alone.

"How 'bout loanin' me a nickel, man?" the leader said.

"I ain't got it."

"Ain't cha goin'nin' da movie?"

"Yeah."

"Den wha'cha mean ya ain't got it? All I find I can have?" He reached toward Stevie's pocket.

Stevie stepped back into a fighting stance and shoved the boy's hand aside. From the edges of his eyes shapes moved.

"Don't worry 'bout yore back," Homer said. "This is just between you and him."

"What are ya supposed to be . . . bad, man?" the leader asked Stevie.

"Bad enough, man."

"I'll see ya 'round," he said and he and his boys stepped back into the alley, glaring as they retreated.

There were three fights that afternoon in the movies. Two between rival gangs and one in the balcony between two gassed head dudes over a girl who left with a third fellow. Homer told Stevie how well he had done with Snoopy and they stayed out of hassles for the remainder of that day.

The rest of the weekend was spent with Homer instructing Stevie in what to look for and how to face it, for trouble was surely coming.

Monday morning was like many others. The dreary succession of junior high school classes passed with the same amount of perverse violence by the students and the exact amount of hate that big city slum schoolteachers can radiate. The erasers thrown at Wild Leo in the third row by the hysterical, horn-rimmed redhead who taught something she said was social functioning; the zigging chalk whistling down the aisle at some pompadoured head in math class; the spitball splattering upon the neck of the shell-shocked English teacher and causing him to verbally fornicate with Jesus; the dragging of Pancho the Spic down to the principal's office for writing obscene suggestions to Rita the Jew; the accumulated deadening hate of packing fifty-one haters in a space that only thirty could possibly fit—Monday morning was like many others.

In this school Stevie had to hide always, had to hide his willingness to learn, his wanting to know and find out. But now, in his second year, he knew how to hide. In his first year he was green and had found himself in fights each week; sometimes three or four in a gang would beat him up as he fought back wildly like a caged animal that didn't have instinct enough to run, even if the gate was opened. These fights usually ended when they hit him in the eyes, blinding him, and then pounded and kicked him to the ground as an added treat to the hundreds of schoolmates jeering the loser.

Force was what the crowd worshiped, Stevie had learned. And for all the many good fights he had provided the mob, hardly anybody acknowledged him as a fighter. Losers are not often kept in mind as long as a year. And there had been no fight for Stevie for over a year, since he had learned to hide so well.

After the lunch hour, the kids formed lines to march back into class. Stevie waited in his line, behind the numerous heads, not thinking of the long afternoon hours ahead, only sucking at the scraps of baloney caught between his teeth from the king-sized hoagie he had eaten at the little lunch counter on Fifth Street.

"Hey, mahthafukker!" a voice at his side said loudly.

Stevie turned his head to see, as did the rest of the kids; it was Snoopy.

"I'll be waitin' fo ya after school, ya little punk," Snoopy warned. "Don't try and git away."

A steady drone teased Stevie's ears the remainder of the afternoon. Guys and girls he didn't know stared at him and pointed and giggled. Some made pantomimed gestures—a bony fist smashing his mouth and the bug-eyed expression of the punch-drunk, a mighty dig to the gut with a boloed right and the resulting doubling up and retching. The mood was intensifying for the afternoon's pagan dance.

18

Those who knew Stevie turned their heads or stayed far from him. Two friends his age from his neighborhood, Brother and Timmy, looked knowingly and smiled and nodded between themselves, sharing this one more defeat of Stevie, whom they had known and seen defeated many other times. A few girls told him how sorry they were and for him to run out the side exit when the bell rang, or even before school ended. Who was Snoopy to create this total terror? he wondered. Stevie was out of his neighborhood, with no strong neighborhood friends to side with him; he had always been an outcast and a foreigner during his school life because the schools closest to him were so "bad." His mother threatened him with boarding school if he was ever compelled to go by the authorities. He constantly lied about his address. So he had nobody there but himself. The Jewish boys he knew and the several Irish, Italian and Polish guys wouldn't mix in a fight among negroes even if one of them was a friend and the other a stranger with a gang to back him up. Fear of the gang was one more reason why he couldn't ask his few friends.

Toward the end of the last period, Stevie raised his hand and asked to be excused from class. A tittering rustle rose about him as he got up and left the room. Inside the boys' toilet his stomach knotted as he sat on the john and tried to think of nothing and keep his legs from trembling, and after a while he straightened his clothes and in the mirror above the washbowl he feinted his left like Homer had shown him over the weekend and shadow-boxed a barrage of hooks and uppercuts into his imaginary opponent's surprised face. He then danced back, waiting for his dream adversary's vicious counter-attack, but stopped him cold with a low right hand thrown belt high as he charged in flailing, and Stevie finally creamed the shadow to the sidewalk with a left bolo to the kidneys. Before he left the cement room he pissed at the urinal, shaking the last drops into his palms and massaging the moist skin for luck.

"Little sucker, you gonna git your ass stomped *today*," Doris said, and he saw the joy of his return on his classmates' faces. "Fool, you should'a got away when ya had the chance," the big girl said when they lined up to leave school.

The fall sky was as gray as a morgue slab, and a pagan dance was held that day, a dance that marked the end and the beginning of something for Stevie Benson. The mob awaited the initiation, jostling and shoving to get better places. All the whites hurried home except for a few from over by the freight yards and from down the waterfront.

When Stevie came out his fire tower exit, two boys bigger than he broke through the line and fell in step with him.

Doris ran up behind.

"Let me hold your coat," she screamed above the gleeful mob.

Stevie pulled his jacket off and put it under his arm.

"Let me hold your coat, little sucker . . . you can't fight with a coat!"

He gave it to her. For blocks they walked, blocks of streets emptied except for Stevie, his two escorts, Doris and the two hundred jostling figures. No one over eighteen stepped from a door; not a teacher or coach or administrator was seen seeking out his car or slinking to a bus stop that day until the dancers upon the concrete were blocks away, souls in time to the trotting and trucking of the savage song of the threshing floor.

Wild Leo screamed and whooped, pushing Pancho the Spic and grabbing leering Rita's hair. Black Delores, her face like a sooted madonna with white rolling eyes, cried real tears, letting the streaks run over her lovely face like rain tracks upon coal. She stayed near but turned away and cried whenever Stevie glanced at her. Brother and Timmy, on the edges of the mob, smirked and stared straight at him when they got their chance.

The parade crossed Eighth Street, then Darien, and at last Ninth waited with a vacant gravel lot across the street from the train bridge. Snoopy squatted there sifting the grit through his fingers with at least ten street fighters around him.

"Dis is gonna be a fair fight, mahthafukker," Snoopy said when he rose and met the party. "I'm gonna kick yore ass until yore nose bleeds, punk." He took off his Eisenhower jacket and shrugged his

20

shoulders to ripple his muscles. "You'll beg yore mama to give you money ta bring ta me, ya understand?"

Stevie remained quiet. A burly boy with a greasy green tam pulled down over his conked head acted as referee. Cheers and squeals rose among the crowd as the referee gave instructions, and pairs of anxious boys began body-punching, the thuds and whacks beating out until the real fight began. Delores stood high on a stoop down the street, framed in the door, as alone as Stevie. Two bobby-socked girls picked up Snoopy's jacket and were on the verge of having a preliminary until the smaller backed down.

The referee pointed to Stevie. "When I say break, punk, you better scratch ass and git back like I tell you or you'll git yore little ass stomped today as well as whupped."

The two came to the center of the circle and began dancing like lightweights. Stevie was indeed an amateur lightweight but had only sparred with the boys in his neighborhood and the club fighters who used the police equipment on weekends. Snoopy's twenty-pound weight edge and his three-year advantage caused him to close fast with Stevie. Stevie won the first exchange by giving the clumsier boy two glancing jolts in the face with his left and right; Snoopy's swing swooshed above the little guy's head. They closed again, immediately, and Stevie tied up his opponent in a clinch and pumped quick shots to the kidneys and gut as he had been taught. Surprised and ashamed at the crowd's wild cheers for the underdog, Snoopy tried to butt him but Stevie had been waiting and dug his head into the taller boy's chest, making him smash his nose. As they broke Stevie hit Snoopy again upon his bloodied nose. And the referee stepped in.

"Here, man," he screamed, talking to Snoopy, "let me take this mahthafukker." He had pulled his sweater off in the late fall weather, and Snoopy stood between him and Stevie as the mob surged out into the street.

"No, no, no, man," Snoopy pleaded. "I can take him. *I can take this little punk any time I want!*"

The rest of the gang whispered among themselves, but Snoopy

wouldn't listen to them when they stepped into the circle with the mob at their heels.

"C'mon, man," Snoopy said to Stevie, pushing his friends back. "It's you and me now, little mahthafukker."

Stevie knew it was his fight and didn't think of anything but winning. No more hiding, no more pulling punches and not talking to the girls at school because he was out of his neighborhood. No more copping out and eating shit. No more, no more! They came for the dance, so now for the floor show. I'm the best, he told himself; I'm the best and today we all find out.

The ring cleared, with even the referee pulled out, and Stevie bobbed and weaved as he pressed in on the dark boy, something he hadn't done before. He jabbed Snoopy four times quickly around the arms and chest and landed once in the throat. He danced, he danced so beautifully, he knew, like to music, like to the sound of drums and clashing cymbals. There was no other place in the universe then for him but that dance floor with every fiber poised and executing an ageless war dance passed down from his father and his father's father before him and the black fathers of his tribe before memory. He danced back, letting Snoopy's swing slip past, and then feinted with his left. Snoopy blinked and then stepped. . . . The gang leader woke up six minutes later with a busted mouth and nose; one eye would be closed shut for two days, and his head would ache for a time because of the mild concussion he received when his skull cracked the curb. Stevie had stood above him for a second after the feint and vicious combination of one, two, three and more jabs pumped into the big boy's face, and then the overhand right, and the step behind the pivot and the hook which smashed into flesh and bone.

He waited for the fallen boy's counterattack.

"Here, mahthafukker," Doris screamed in the stunned second. "Run, mahthafukker, run . . . *run!*"

Stevie took his coat thrown at him and sped through the crowd behind him, speeding past smiling pearly-toothed Delores, running down the hill toward home. Running like he had never run in his life. All of Snoopy's boys seemed to be fifty steps behind, and behind

22

them was the insane mob, crazy from the smash performance and lusting for added gore.

At the corner, an old Hudson turned and Stevie grabbed the door handle and leaped inside.

"What the hell?" the driver started, but the exhausted boy pointed back and one look through the rear-view mirror gave the driver incentive to tramp on the gas.

After a week of negotiations between Homer and Snoopy, and missing days at school, with a couple of running fights between Snoopy's boys and the ones Homer sent to escort Stevie back to his territory, the thing settled, and Brother and Timmy said, "You won!" and nodded their heads as they passed.

The following week Doris took Stevie to her house after school and ordered her little brother out. Then she showed Stevie how to really have sex, the way grownups did.

They met at her place every day after school for over a month. She told him about the big guys she had at night, real men, she said, some even fathers and husbands that she had whenever she wanted. It seemed to Stevie that it was always she who wanted them from her way of telling it, and refused if they made demands upon her. She lived on the top floor of a tenement and one day when Stevie was between her large dark thighs, his teeth nibbling at her earlobe the way she had shown him as they grunted and strained, they heard a loose step crack. He jumped up and ran to the window and Doris pulled down her dress just as her girl friend pushed the door open and walked in.

"Don't ya know how to knock, bitch?" Doris growled.

"I've never had to before. . . . Was I interruptin' somethin'?" the girl asked. She was taller than Doris and almost as old. She was a grade ahead of both Stevie and Doris, and she and Doris ran around with a gang that called themselves the Controlerellas.

"How are you, Chuckie?" the girl asked Stevie. In this part of town he had a different nickname.

"Okay," he said over his shoulder.

He watched out the window. His fly had been buttoned just in time but the front of his pants pushed out. He peered from the window as the girls talked, watching the trolley and the cars go down Tenth Street, and the people on the streets that day, and looking south he saw the tall PSFS building rising from the gray dust of the slums, towering above them as if the structure's foundation was planted in the muck of the ghetto.

The street below looked small to Stevie and innocent, but he knew it was one of the main trails in the jungle. He liked being up high looking down at the people. He liked being there with Doris, even though she bullied him in public; she was nice to him when they were alone, and best of all she said she liked the way he did it to her because he was young and strong and it took him a long time to finish.

"Give me a cigarette, Chuck," Doris's friend said.

He turned his head away from the window; she was smiling.

"Give me a cigarette, boy!"

He walked over to the couch and handed her a cigarette from his pack. She shrieked with laughter as she snatched it and leaned across Doris, choking and coughing. Stevie peeped down at his pants front.

He always betrayed himself, he knew. Always.

"Give me one too," Doris said. She snatched the entire pack from his hands. "You don't need any, you silly little bastard."

Her friend laughed even louder.

Doris let him come to see her two more afternoons, but the times after that day of discovery, when he asked to be let up her stairs she told him no, though sometimes she would let him kiss her hurriedly in her vestibule. She stopped coming to school and the kids gossiped that she had been thrown out because of being pregnant.

The week before she died Stevie and Homer were on Hutchinson Street, close to where Doris lived. They waited outside a girl's house who they were going to walk back to their neighborhood for a party. As they waited, Doris walked through the narrow streets with her tall thin friend.

24

"Hey, lil mahthafukker," she yelled to Stevie, "whatcha doin' up this way?" She stopped, placing her hands on overblown hips, and stared at him through shiny eyes. "You know we don't allow little pricks up here."

She was loud and evil-sounding like the times at school when she threatened the boys, so Stevie knew she wasn't serious.

"Just hangin' out," he answered.

"Whatcha been doin' lately?" she asked.

"Just eatin' fried chicken and fukkin' ev'va night, baby," he said, saying the line of the street song with a smile.

The girls flounced off in hobbling skirts and jeered at him to get out of "their" territory and swung their behinds in huge circles down the street, laughing, stumbling and swearing.

"Whatcha let that whore speak ta ya like that fo, man?" Homer had said. "You should'a punched that black bitch in da mouf."

Dandy had never told anyone about Doris. She had been his first, the first that mattered, for he had been playing sex games among the tenements since he was seven, but Doris had been the one who had made him feel for the first time that something which frightened and was vital to him. The only times before the quick afternoons with Doris on her couch were when he had had dreams he couldn't make out but he awoke afterwards on his belly, wet and scared.

Since the first day with Doris he had sought out at least ten other girls. Slum girls who waited for any show of affection, especially from one their own age with a smooth brown face and who knew what to do. Dandy's challenge to Doris hadn't been entirely groundless, even though sweet black Delores would only let him love her from across the aisle. He was out in the street every night. He knew Doris wanted to see him after the encounter on the side street, and her boisterous smile made him sweat some as he promised to go see her, for his feelings for the girl had grown suddenly proportional to his pants front, which moved out as he thought of her luscious warmth. He didn't make it to her place that week. The next, Doris died shortly after missing a fire net drawn under the window of her burning apartment.

Dandy stopped by to see her little brother some weeks later and they both whispered of her and cried without thinking of being manly.

". . . and by the grace of God . . . Ahhhmen," Uncle Clyde intoned.

"Pass the biscuits," Roy said.

"Just wait a minute, boy," Richard ordered and acted cross and older than he was. "Shouldn't be so greedy!"

"Hush up, you two little boys," Ida James said. "All the way back from Sister Ossie Mae's you been at it."

"Yeah, keep quiet, you little boys," Uncle Clyde said with a mouth filled with food.

"Here, Dandy," Ida said and poured his lemonade for him.

"Why, looky dere . . . old Dandy's makin' out like a madman," Jack Bowen slurred.

"Marie Ann, ya better look out or Ida will be takin' Dandy away from you," Roy said.

Marie shrugged and shoveled a spoonful of beans into her mouth. "Nobody's studden 'bout Dandy."

"Dandy, your city ways don't seem to be workin' any on Marie Ann," Aunt Bessie said. "What's wrong, boy?" She prodded Dandy, for she knew that he was working on her favorite and he would have her if he got the chance.

"I don't know," Dandy answered. "I guess she thinks I'm a slicker."

"Hee hee heee . . ." Roy chortled. "Oooeee . . . hee heee . . ."

"Eat your supper, boy!"

"Well, that's what you is, boy." Jack drawled and slipped tenses and syntax. "One of dem dere city slickers, and mah lil sister ain'ta gonna be fooled none any by y'all kind, *boy.*" He made a private joke, though secretly he wanted his sister and Dandy to be friendlier. Dandy would make a pretty fair brother-in-law, he thought, and he felt that any man who ever touched her would *have* to marry Marie Ann.

26

"Why are you so quiet, Sister Ida?" Uncle Clyde asked.

"Not much ta say, Unc' Clyde."

Ida was a stocky yellow girl who had been turned out by her mother after her father had taken her for over a period of two years and at last had succeeded in giving her his son. She was a ward of the state from being a minor and for having made herself available to any man in her town, forty miles south of Mary's Shore, who had the courage to talk to the fifteen-year-old for over five minutes. Many had the guts and word finally got around to the authorities that a girl and baby were living in an abandoned shack close to town, and there were all sorts of carryings-on. The powers couldn't charge Ida with anything more than vagrancy since she never asked for money from her numerous visitors, and not even vag stuck when it was found she was a teen-ager, though she seemed ten years older, or so it was assumed. Ida didn't talk much and Dandy suspected that she was a bit dense since she was relieved that her baby had been taken from her. But she had enough sense to slip him a note his first day there that her heart was just about to actually burst from love of him.

She worked each day on a neighboring farm watching children or helping in the kitchen, for at least one member of each family in Mt. Holy had to go into town or farther to jobs in outlying districts. Some drove even to Dover and to Wilmington in Delaware.

Dandy knew his turn would come with Ida. Jack had told him how he would get her when he had the chance, not knowing that Dandy also schemed on her stubby flanks, for they both were sure that Ida James was as hot and ready as a ten-cent pistol.

"Dandy," Uncle Clyde asked. "When you comin' out with me or one of the boys on the job?"

"Anytime, Uncle Clyde. How 'bout tomorrow?"

"Clyde, you know that boy don't want to work," Aunt Bessie said. She rubbed it in about Dandy being able to pay his board without working, for Dandy's mother had a civil service job in the city, and the city slick Dandy was from Philly and had taken piano lessons and boxing lessons and singing and dancing lessons, and had a motorcycle (really only a motorbike). He was her current status symbol.

"No, he probably can't pull himself away from Marie Ann," Ida said and peeped over her fork at the other girl across the table.

"I wish he could go somewheres," Marie Ann said. "I'm sure tired of lookin' at him."

The remainder of the table, except for Uncle Clyde, entered the conversation and bet about which of the girls would get Dandy, and the dinner ended with Aunt Bess promising that if anybody got Marie Ann they would go immediately to jail, whether or not they used "protection."

"NOW, BESSIE, YOU KNOW YOU SHOULDN'T BE TALKIN' LIKE DAT IN FRONT OF DESE HARE KIDS," Uncle Clyde hollered, nearly upsetting his greens.

"Well, all of them are big enough to take care of themselves, and none of mine ain't goin' 'round dumb for most of their lives, especially about somethin' that everybody has got ta do . . . or at least should try once, Clyde."

"Oh, hush up, woman."

"Well, I've told them already and even given them money to get 'em with," the old woman said. "All they have ta do is come and ask and I'll give them money to buy them. I ain't takin' the blame if somethin' happens. I'll tell the world it ain't Bessie's fault."

"You talk too much, Bessie."

It was a good dinner.

After dinner, Dandy went to the trailer and poured hog feed into two large slop buckets and then carried them outside to the pig barrel. Setting the buckets down, he lifted the large ladle and began filling a scoop at a time. The dogs had been tied for their evening feed, given by Roy coaxing and wheedling with puckered lips and many "Here, boys" to the already leashed animals. As Dandy started on the second bucket Marie Ann and Ida came out of the house and they tugged at each other until one got the last tag; then Marie began trotting over toward the henhouse, where the outhouse stood.

"I'm goin' to get you when ya come back, Marie Ann," Ida called out.

"Ya know what you'll git, Ida," she said, turning around and making a fist and showing where on the light girl's face she would plant it. "And that goes double for your friend Dandy," she said before she entered the closetlike building.

Ida skipped over to the trailer and went inside. Dandy submerged the edge of the ladle in the thick broth and pulled it out with sucking sounds, pouring the mixture in the nearly filled last bucket. He heard the cracked corn rattling in the pan Ida used to feed the chickens.

"Come here, Dandy, I want ta show ya somethin'," she said from inside the trailer.

Dandy saw Roy cross the yard from the horse compound, and he stirred the pigs' food until the boy was gone into the house.

"Dandy?"

Inside the trailer he found Ida in a dim corner and kissed her thick moist lips.

"I told Marie Ann that I loved you and she got mad."

"No, she didn't. You know that she likes Junior Kane."

"She did so get mad."

"She was teasin' you."

"No, she weren't and she better not!"

"We better go," Dandy said after a while. "Someone will be out here looking for us."

"Okay. I have ta go ta choir rehearsal tonight but I want ta talk ta ya when I git back."

Marie Ann was humming a hymn when Dandy passed the back of the outhouse with the heavy buckets.

The pigs were always ready to feed. No matter how Dandy filled their troughs to brimming, when he returned the next day all had been swilled up and nothing remained but the stained, weathered boards of the troughs. When he turned the buckets up and splashed the food into the troughs, the pigs made oinking sounds which he had never gotten used to. He watched the fat beasts feeding, pushing each other aside, and remembered the story he had read of a man who had lain helpless in a pigpen and had been eaten alive.

On the way back to the house, climbing the stubbled trail beside

29

the nearly grown summer corn, he saw three buzzards carried through the sky in the streams of invisible forces which he had been told were air currents. He found Jack Bowen waiting for him halfway up the rise.

"Well, howdy dowdy, Bowen?"

"Well, how yawhl doin', Mr. Benson?"

Jack was four years older than Dandy, but he allowed the younger boy to carry on rituals and treated him as an equal.

"How the girls treatin' ya, Bowen?" Dandy asked.

"Dey ain't treatin' one bit, partner, not a'tall."

Jack Bowen was more intelligent than Dandy; if he could break away from the farm and the series of mill-hand, packing-plant-helper jobs, he could be saved, Dandy knew but could not tell his friend. Jack lived as much for the future as for payday; he was forever participating in national contests that promised trips to Paris and mink coats and an occasional Cadillac. He purposely exaggerated his drawl, though he could speak better than Dandy could then; he could tell stories like nobody else, and knew more about science, math and those subjects' vocabularies. Dandy had never heard Jack's actual plans except once.

It was a day in early July that Jack took Dandy to the chicken plant to get a job. Buddy Henderson drove them across the state line into Delaware, where he and his girl worked. Buddy's girl, Betty Sue, was from Florida and chewed tobacco and wore men's pants because she had done so much field work she didn't "rightly take to dresses no mo'," and she couldn't read nor write much aside her name, Betty Sue. She had been living since spring in the shack village of itinerant workers behind the Hamilton tomato packing plant, until Buddy had gotten her to housekeep with him.

The foreman hired everyone that day, for truckloads of birds waited to be slaughtered.

Dandy's job was to hang the chickens by their feet, pulling them from the crates as they flapped, squawked and pecked, and attaching the victims to metal clamps swinging under the conveyor. The belt

30

ran, one clamp which had to be filled after another, and two farm boys worked beside Dandy and showed him how inadequate he was at hanging chickens at six bits an hour.

Sitting in a chair, ten feet down the line from Dandy, was an old fat man who cut the chickens' white throats. The man was black and wore a black rubber apron; the bib shielded his chest, the straps climbed up over his white-shirted shoulders and blended like dark bands with his neck. Dandy emptied crate after crate of white leghorns and sent them cackling down to the busy man with the blade. Sometimes a brown bird or a black with gray and white speckles found its way among the snowy ones and they added contrast, floating upended toward the chair, their red wattles dangling, then the brief last scream as one black hand reached out and anchored the head, and then the other hand moved, bringing red of a more alive hue streaming over their throats.

That lunch hour Dandy sat with Jack and Buddy Henderson and Betty Sue, eating homemade sandwiches of baloney and peanut butter.

"Hope ta gawd dese hare chickens hold out another two munts," Buddy remarked.

"I wouldn't care none if'in dey cut every last one's of da sonsabitches' throats nex' hour," Jack said. "There ain't no future bein' a chicken-plucker."

"Beats not eatin'," Buddy said. "Whatcha do if dere were no job in da chicken plant nor any in da 'maters or any work a'tall?"

"Well, I don't know 'bout chaw, Buddy boy," Jack drawled, "but one ah dese hare days I'm hoppin' dat old Greyhound out on da road an' goin' up ta Philly an' git me ah job in da big post office up dere."

"Sheet, nigger," Betty Sue said. "When's de last time ya ev'va seen some nigger in a white shirt in da post office? Dey got jest de job fo all ya white-shirt niggers right here."

Jack didn't say anything for the rest of the lunch period, just munched his biscuit bread and peanut butter and looked mean. Everyone knew he would probably never go north to his post office job.

31

Jack Bowen didn't seem like most brothers to Dandy. He didn't make threats or get angry when Marie Ann first showed interest in Dandy. Lots of times Jack would daydream aloud with Dandy. He would tell how he would one day visit Dandy in the city, and maybe not go back to Mary's Shore. Secretly, Dandy knew Jack dreamed of visiting him and Marie Ann in their home in the wonderful city. But, nevertheless, they were real friends; they had mutual enemies.

"That goddamned Uncle Clyde is goin' ta git it one day," Jack said.

"What happened?"

"Wahl, he just rides me, that's all. I was on the second floor of the mill today stackin' boxes like Mr. Harvey Wentley told me and Uncle Clyde came on up there and pulled me off the job."

"Yeah? That sounds bad."

"Sho nuf, hope ma gonna die but Harvey like ta pitched a bitch when he saw me traipsin' my pretty black self down there on the mill floor amongst all them white gals."

"Yeah, I hear he don't like none of the young fellows ta be down dere near the girls, not even with himself dere."

"That's sho is right. Uncle Clyde is harmless—that's why he's foreman—but if he don't always stop fukkin' wit' me . . . I'm goin' ta knock his ole rusty ass off."

They neared the rear of the outhouse and fell silent because they didn't know who might be inside.

After they passed, Jack said, "Junior Kane is comin' over, gonna go ov'va ta his place for some boozin' tonight."

"Yeah?"

"How 'bout goin'?"

"Why, sho nuf, Mr. Bowen."

Junior Kane had a '34 Chevy and three half-sisters. The girls were young enough for Dandy and all attractive in their big-eyed, slow-talkin' country ways. Their reputations were of being fast girls for that part of the world.

Jack pulled out a pack of Chesterfields. He offered Dandy one and they lit up. Dandy didn't like to smoke. Before he began training, he smoked just enough to let his gang know that he did and after, he almost stopped completely. Since he had come down to Mt. Holy on his second vacation, he smoked whenever offered.

They walked into the kitchen, cigarettes in mouths. Uncle Clyde and Aunt Bessie were fussing.

"Now when I tell these little boys ta do somethin', Bessie, I meant it, ya hear?"

"These kids ain't for you to be always jumpin' on whenever you get ready, Clyde."

Marie Ann stood beside the sink with a dish towel and gave approving looks to Aunt Bessie. Ida was over the sink with elbows in suds, softly singing a gospel song.

Jack and Dandy crept through the kitchen, crossed the front room and climbed to their room on the second floor. They passed Marie Ann and Ida's room first, then a spare room that was used when more guests arrived or during camp meeting times when the house was jammed, and reached their large room at the end of the hall, which ran the length of the house and had four large beds and a double-decker that Roy and Richard preferred to sleep in.

Jack stretched out on his bed and Dandy sat on his, reaching for a Western magazine on the nightstand between them.

"The Durango Kid sure gits into it, don't he?" Dandy commented.

Jack peered over his arms and said, "Sho do. I couldn't put that book there down until I had found out how the showdown would come off."

A tramping upon the stairs was heard.

"Stop it, Fatso." A cry came before the speeding tumble of tennis shoes.

"Hee heee heee . . ."

Roy and Richard burst around the corner at the stairs' top, and Richard chased the giggling boy down the hallway into the bedroom.

Roy pulled himself into a corner between wall, bureau and bed, and Richard, like a small scarecrow, thrashed at him with halfhearted pokes of his fists.

"Heee heee . . . Oooo, man," Roy called to his antagonist. "Fatso, stop!"

"Yeah, stop it, goddammit," Jack shouted.

"Oh, Bo," his brother protested. "Bo, he's always botherin' me."

"Heee . . . Dat ain't right, Bowen," Roy said.

"SHUT UP, BOTH OF YOU! I DON'T WANT TA HEAR ANY MORE OF IT!"

Richard stepped away from the hole where Roy crouched and grumbled as he searched through a drawer. Roy came out, hand over mouth, strangling on his laughs, and finally hid his head under the double-decked bed, pretending to look for shoes.

"You guys goin' to choir meetin'?" Dandy asked the younger boys.

"Yeah, Dandy," Richard said. "We goin' but I don't know if'in we'll stay in the choir."

"Fatso's startin' a quartet," Roy spoke out.

"A quartet?" Jack said. "What makes ya think ya can sing?"

"Well, it's like dis, Bo," one of them began. And they took the next half hour while changing their clothes to describe the gospel quartet they were starting and how when they were good enough their group, "The Mt. Holy Four," would go on nationwide tours, even to New York City and Philly.

"Why don't you come on out and try to get on at the mill tomorrow, Dandy?" Jack said after the boys had gone downstairs.

"Oh, I'd like ta, Jack, but you remember the kiddin' I got when I quit the chicken plant after three days."

"Awww, forgit that," Jack said. "Remember I quit two days later."

"Yeah, but you work all the time and I don't even have ta unless I want ta have extra money."

"I know, but you're gittin' pretty tired 'round here all day listenin' to Bessie. . . . Say, are ya makin' much time with mah little sister?" There was a guarded flash in his eyes.

"Nawh, not much," Dandy said. "Aunt Bessie is around all da time."

34

"Well, ya shouldn't mind comin' down ta da plant then. Thar's ah couple ah nice gals down there, and you can always take Marie Ann ta the movies in Dover on Saturday nights."

"I'll ask Aunt Bessie."

A car chugged into the driveway; its wheezing engine clanged in time to the barks and yips and prancing of the newly unleashed dogs. The car's horn went *ahhh hunnggaaa ahhh hunnggaaa ahhh hunnggaaa* before the brittle pinging of the girls' giggles rose above Aunt Bessie's voice bellowing welcomes to Junior Kane from the kitchen window.

Downstairs, Dandy stopped in the kitchen with Aunt Bess and Uncle Clyde as Jack strolled out to the car surrounded by the girls and the two small boys on the old running boards.

"Howdy dere, Bowen," the driver yelled.

"Wahl, if'n it ain't dat mule thief, Bro Kane."

The girls laughed more; their soft and syrupy drawls oozed over the heavy evening air as the sky glowed pink and violet, and above trees to the east, twilight was promised by the gleam of a full moon on a pale blue-purple horizon.

"I'm goin' down ta the mill with Jack tomorrow, Aunt Bessie," Dandy said.

"Okay, son," the old woman answered.

"Wha' ya say, Dandy?" the old man asked.

"I'm goin' ta try an' get on at da mill, Uncle Clyde."

"Shssucks . . . who you tryin' ta fool, boy? You don't wan' ta work."

"Ain't none of your business, Clyde," Aunt Bess said.

"Oh, dammit, Bessie! I don't care what he does but he better know he's gonna work when he's on mah crew. I don't play no favorites."

"We know you don't play favorites, Clyde," the woman said. "You'd work your mamma to death if that white man wanted ya."

"Now lissen here, Bessie!"

Dandy went out the door and over to the car. Jack sat in the front next to the driver and the remainder of the group stood by the windows.

"Howdy dere, Dandy," the driver said.

"Hi, Junior."

"What's goin' on with you, Dandy?"

"Wahl, I guess I'll be workin' with you guys startin' tomorrow."

Excitement rose, with everyone having something to add about Dandy's decision. Finally, Marie Ann went into the house, soon followed by Ida.

"Ain't you boys goin' ta choir rehearsal?" Dandy asked.

"Yeah, we goin' as soon as Ida gits ready. Shucks, she's been out hare makin' eyes at Junior Kane hare an' makin' us late."

Junior was a sun-darkened wiry boy in his late teens. He spoke with a coarse accent and laughed a lot.

"Stop dat fibbin'," Jack said. "You knows Marie Ann has got Junior all staked out." Dandy saw Jack wink at him from behind Junior Kane's head. Junior broke into a great grin and showed tobacco-stained teeth.

"But, Bo!" one of the little boys protested.

"Shut up! Don't let me hear anything 'bout nobody flirtin' wit' Marie Ann's boyfriend."

"Here she comes."

Ida came out of the house wearing a red full-length coat. The hue heightened her bright skin and caused her teeth to flash within the scarlet-smeared mouth. She waved at Aunt Bessie through the kitchen-door window and turned toward the car and her admirers.

"See you, Junior," she said and waved. "See you when I git home, Dandy and Bo." She hurried down the drive. "Come on, you little boys," she called while the two pups wagged their ends behind her heels.

"I'll race ya to Ida, Fatso."

"Oooo, man, we better catch her before she gets by the cemetery, or Aunt Bess will get on us."

And the boys were gone down the drive, laughing and squealing to the mingled barking of the dogs and the threatening yells of Ida.

Dandy opened the rear door and crawled in the back.

"Want a cigarette, Dandy?" Junior offered.

"Wow, a Raleigh!"

"Yeah, I save the coupons."

The radio played country music.

> Rocks are mah cradle . . . da cole ground's mah bed . . .
> da highway's mah home and I's might as well be
> dead . . .

Night came soon and the lights shone from the kitchen window and upstairs in Marie Ann's room. From under the seat Junior pulled four quarts of beer and opened each with a minimum of fizzing and handed Jack and Dandy one bottle.

"Ohhheee, Kane, you're really goin' ta do it tonight, boy," Jack said.

"Them sisters of mine have got some home brew ready and we might as well git primed."

> Thar I go . . . thar I go . . . thaaare I goo'oh . . . purty baby
> you's 's de soul that snaps mah control . . .

Marie Ann came out of the house wearing fresh short shorts and a white blouse outlining her young breasts.

"Ya ready ta go, Marie?" Junior asked as she got in the back of the car next to Dandy.

"Nawh, I didn't go ta choir meetin' and I better not go with yawhl."

"Why not, Marie? Jack will be dere." Junior handed her the last quart of beer and she peered into the kitchen window to see if the old folks sat at the table. Aunt Bess and Uncle Clyde were in the front of the house; they sat in their bedroom off the living room or watched television. Marie sipped at the beer. "Damn, this is good." She leaned her elbows across the top of the front seat and placed her head between the half-turned heads of her brother and her boyfriend, Junior Kane.

"Sho gits dark quick around here," she said.

And night was outside, enclosing the blackened car as the pitter-patter of the returning dogs' feet came from the road, and the cricket music and an occasional pig's oink and a drowsy duck quacking at the dark, while the white summer moon swung up into the black, star-pierced southern heavens, and the stars that no city lights dimmed winked as if they too had secrets.

> Wha ain't ya out in da forest fightin' dose grea' big ole grizzly bears?
> I's a lady!
> Dey got lady bears out dere.

"Dandy, you'll like it down the mill," Jack said.

"Ya sho will, boy," Junior Kane said. "Mr. Harvey Wentley's sho nice ta git along wit'."

"I'm sho glad yo goin', Dandy," Marie Ann teased. "Get real tired ah seein' yo face 'round here all the time."

Dandy's hand moved across the seat and caressed her bare legs; she flinched but took another sip of beer. Dandy had his bottle between his knees and drew on one of the cigarettes he took from Junior.

"Ya gonna buy me one of them great big straw hats when ya git paid, Dandy?" Marie asked.

"One ah them Texas ones . . . shore will, Marie. I don't want ya ta git any blacker," he teased. "I'll git one with a string on it so ya can drop it back over ya neck and let ya hair fly."

"Ya never asked me fo ah ten-gallon straw hat, Marie Ann," Junior said.

And the music played.

> I found mah thrill on Blueberry Hill . . . on Blueberry Hill
> . . . where I found you . . .

"How's Ethel gittin' along?" Jack asked Junior.

"Oeewee, she's fit to be tied. Daisy and Helen came down ta da mill, ya know, and got on. Now dere camp meetin' outfits gonna be as purty as hers."

38

"Sho nuff?" Jack said.

"Hee heee . . ." Marie Ann simpered.

"Ah most like ta died too when I heard, Marie," Junior said.

"Ahm jest glad I don't have ta work . . . got mah ole big bro here," she said and caressed her brother's arm.

Dandy's fingers in the dark had crawled under the band of her shorts and squeezed between the firm thighs and around between the soft lips of the swelling labia. She squirmed and hunched nearer her boyfriend and rested her head upon her brother's shoulder.

"What y'all keep gigglin' fo, Marie Ann?" Junior Kane asked.

"This is really some good beer," she said as she willed herself to restrain the shudder which reached from her center, and she opened her legs wide in the near-total blackness and rested the rear end of her tight bottom on the cushion and leaned fully forward with her knees bent and her arms supporting herself.

"Give me a cigarette, Junior, pleez," she asked.

"I didn't know you did all this, gal," Junior kidded and giggled with her as he fished for his pack.

Marie Ann stretched farther over so that the light of the match would not reach over the rim of the car seat, and Dandy's moist moving finger flickered over her pursy clitoris.

"Ummm . . ." she said and hunched even farther forward.

"Wha you say, Marie?" Junior Kane asked.

"Just thinkin' . . ." she said.

Dandy took another long swallow of his beer, nearly finishing the bottle. Jack tilted his up and Junior got bold enough to twist about and kiss Marie Ann full in the mouth.

"Ummm . . ." she said between her lips, and Dandy's finger worked like a lever. "Ohhh . . . that's so good," she said as Junior pressed harder. Dandy wondered how the two in front could not detect the heavy sweet funk odor.

"Whatcha doin' ta mah baby sister?" Jack Bowen kidded in the dark. "Dandy, boy, you sittin' back dere and lettin' Junior git away with the goods."

"Yeah, Junior's really makin' out," Dandy said.

39

"Shusss . . . ooeee . . . ummm . . ." Marie said and wriggled too much and lifted her girlish rear fully off the back seat.

"Owww . . . Marie Ann," Junior Kane cried. "You know how ta French kiss. Where did ya larn ta use yo tongue like dat?"

"Okay, children," Jack spoke up and put his hand on Junior's shoulder. "That's enough for tonight."

Marie Ann sat back and gave a convulsive tremble as she lowered herself fully upon Dandy's hand.

"Wha'cha shiverin' fo, Marie?" Junior asked as she grabbed his hands and arm. "Bowen," he called out. "Dis y'ere lil beer's got dis gal high as a Georgia pine."

And the radio never stopped.

> Mah pappa's a jockey an he teach me how ta ride . . .
> Oh, yeah, mah pappa's a jockey an he teach me how ta
> ride . . . He said git in da middle son an' ya move from
> side to side . . .

"I have ta go," Marie said. She jerked across the seat and stepped out. "Good night, Dandy."

"Good night, Marie Ann," Junior called.

"Night, Junior."

The screen door slapped shut and the boys in the car were quiet. A pig squealed from the pens and the darkness chirped with crickets.

> I's wan' ah bowlegg'd w'man dat's all . . . I's wan ah
> bowlegg'd woman dat's tall . . .

"Sho was a good starter fo tonight," Junior said and lifted the last of his beer. "Here's the rest of Marie's, Dandy, why don't ya finish it?"

"Thanks, partner."

"Wahl, let's be gittin' whare we ain't," Jack urged.

"Okay thar," Junior yelled and turned on the ignition.

"Wahl, that leaves me out, fellows," Dandy said and stepped into the yard. The dogs trotted up to him and wagged their tails in the moonlight, their eyes glistening yellow in the dark.

40

"Wha'cha say, Dandy?" Junior asked. "I thought ya was comin' wit' us."

"Can't. Startin' at the mill tomorrow and the first day is always hell. It's almost eight now and I'll have ta get up at five-thirty."

"Shit," Jack said. "So do we."

"Yeah, but you're use'ta it."

"Awww, c'mon, Dandy. I promised Helen I would bring ya back. She's fixin' up all fo ya," Junior said.

"Nawh . . . can't do it. I'll see her tomorrow at work and explain."

. . . wit' her big bowlegs so wide apart . . .

The taillights of the '34 Chevy dipped up the road as the old car banged over potholes. Dandy entered the house and looked back through the screen at the two red lights jerking away.

"Good night, Uncle Clyde," Dandy said as he passed the old man sitting before the television screen, the set almost booming.

"I thought you were goin' with Jack and Junior," the old man said. "Your Aunt Bessie went ta sleep because she thought everybody was out."

"Nawh, have ta start work in the morning, so I better get some sleep."

"Wahl, son . . . I didn't know ya had dat much sense."

The old woman slept, Dandy thought, because she didn't know anyone would be home but her and the old man. If she had known that Marie and he would be alone . . .

Dandy passed the girls' room; doorless, the entrance framed Marie lying face down upon the bed with her head toward the window.

Dandy went to his room and untied his shoes and let them drop loudly upon the floor. Then he undressed and changed into his pajamas. Later, with lights out, he tiptoed down the hallway and into the girls' room.

"Dandy, no!" Marie whispered when he turned her over on her back.

He put his finger to his lips and then tiptoed back to the door and clicked off the light. Moonlight spilled over the girl, her white blouse catching the light and showing dark valleys below her breasts.

"No, Dandy," she whispered. *"Aunt Bess will hear."*

"She's asleep!"

"Uncle Clyde!"

"You know he can't hear so good."

"No, Dandy, I can't," she murmured as he unbuttoned her shorts and pulled them with her panties down over her knees, down her brown moon-revealed thighs, down her long night-exposed legs to her tennis shoes.

She clamped her feet tight. Dandy tried to pry them apart, but she held them with all her strength and he couldn't get them apart unless he forced her with all his power.

The moonlight moved down over her brown body. Dandy moved up and kissed her lips as she rolled her head from side to side, and he kissed her shut eyes as she rolled her head, the muscles taut in her neck, and finally, after the pure white blouse was gone and the brassiere, he suckled her breasts in his starved mouth as her head shook no no no no no.

"No, Dandy, you gonna com' in me!"

"No, darling, I'll use protection," he said. *"Don't you understand I love you. I'll take care of you. Trust me!"*

"I'm sorry, Dandy. I can't. I just can't. I'm so sorry!"

Half an hour later, twin tear streaks running from Marie's eyes caught the moonlight and dripped into her matted hair and dampened the pillows and spread, and Dandy felt like adding to the deluge, for he had gotten no further in his conquest than inserting the same practiced finger and making the girl's dark nipples stand out like buttons. His finger worked and his lips worked kissing away the tears and warming the tight eyelids and peppering the little nipples with pecks. His lips also pleaded in low prayer to the beautiful brown animal, and his eyes helped by the full moon fixed for moments on the curling pubic hair above his hand.

42

"Ahm sorry, Dandy; don't be mad at me. . . . Will ya still git me the Texas hat?"

And the video still blared below.

Tonight we bring you the passionate saga of love and . . .

When Richard and Roy and Ida climbed the stairs to their bedrooms, Dandy had rolled Marie under the covers but had done little else.

"Good night," Aunt Bessie called up. "Is everybody home now?"

"Yes, ma'm," Ida replied. "All 'cept'n Bo and Dandy."

"I'm goin' ta be da greatest lead tenor on da Eastern Shore," Roy promised.

"Awww, man, you ain't gonna be nothin'," Richard said as they passed the girls' doorway. "A chicken can crow better den you."

"Shut up, you little boys," Ida warned and stepped into her room. "Don't be makin' a lot of fuss."

"Don't turn that light on, Ida," Marie Ann said.

The moon had been lost somewhere above the Mt. Holy church steeple when Jack Bowen crept up the stairs, slipped past his sister's and Ida's room and sat on his bed.

"Damn . . ." he said. "Where's Dandy?"

"Heee . . . heee . . ."

"Wha ya say, Roy?" he asked.

"Yeah, Bo . . . heee heee . . ."

"Oooo, man, shut up," Richard warned.

"Well, I'll be damned," Jack said softly and slipped under the covers.

Down the hall, the bed in the girls' room squeaked barely when a violent movement was made.

"Ohhh . . . ohhh . . . Dandy," Ida James whimpered. *"I love you."*

"Shusss . . ." he shushed her.

Marie Ann whimpered in her sleep, a captive in a bad dream, and beside her Dandy clutched the big yaller hot-as-a-ten-cent-pistol-gal

43

to himself and worried about how he would tell Jack Bowen in the morning that he had never touched his baby sister.

That country time was years ago, I thought later that night when thinking again of the boy called Dandy, while seated in a lonely seat within the plunging "V" trolley car, rocking through the vacant Vermont Avenue blocks, the conductor passing the hours with the sound of blues on his tiny transistor. The steel electric monster swayed and sped past stop after empty stop without halting. Speeding without stopping almost as my mind sped back to the past and drew again forward to the present and paused, as from a hesitant fingertip released from a switch, as if the pressure was instinctively relaxed at each intersection, to gather recollections of a life fast slipping by like lights outside my lighted vehicle's black window.

Dandy lived years ago in his own past, in places of black summer nights swollen by romantic illusions of youth and love, and of even darker girls not yet bulging with their full pregnant portents but then surging with dark pleasures. Years ago and miles ago, and many black nights since have I waited to end in loneliness and sometimes in clinging to other Maries and Idas and Dorises. Long ago. So once ago. Long long and so far ago. Night and life seemed to be ending almost as rapidly as the trip on the rapid electric car speeding north toward Hollywood.

The drinks had made a difference when Ernest and I had passed the beer and wine around at Len's. Lou had brightened and glowed after her first beer and Olu became an accomplished twister. Connie had begged off at first but with our coaxing had taken a glass of wine and shortly afterwards began giggling and talking brokenly to whoever she was near.

Ernest and I drank steadily, changing records and flipping through the magazines and books. The drinks made the difference with the night outside black against the panes, and the colored lights within the strange room altering the scene, since dark had fallen, into a surreal cavern.

44

The trolley stopped at Washington and an old dumpy woman boarded. She dropped her quarter into the fare box and sniffed at the driver's choice of music as she headed toward the rear. She took the seat in front of me and turned her head from side to side and mumbled to herself.

Her face resembled a hound's, sagging and solemn with bags and pouches. The skin was flecked and hairs and moles sprouted. A long gray dress covered her legs. She wore no coat in the night.

"You goin' all way to the end of the line?" she asked, turning partially about.

"Yeah," I said.

"Well, I ain't. Gettin' off at Wilshire."

The trolley snarled up the hill to Venice and then dropped down the easy descent to the asphalt valley where Olympic bit through the crest like an empty riverlet.

The buildings changed from the black ghetto types, and more filled dim shopwindows looked out into the deserted street.

"Do you go to school?" she asked.

"Yeah."

"I always wanted ta go ta school. Couldn't. Too many of us so I got married. Married no-count Tom. Four kids. Three boys and ah no-count girl like her no-count daddy."

"Where your sons?"

She turned farther around and almost breathed into my face. A chalky dust clung to her jaws and a bead of snot dribbled down her top lip. Her eyes were dreary and her hair matted over her brow.

"All mah boys are dead and gone 'cept'n for one. . . . One got killed in the war . . . he were a good boy. 'n' the nex' just died like his no-good daddy. The last one is back east. The youngest and he's no-count. Won't even write. Almost as bad as his sister."

"That's too bad," I said.

"Do ya 'member the Depression?"

"Yeah," I replied. "Some. The very last part before the war, but I was too young to know what it was all about. I just thought everybody lived like we did. . . . You know, I've eaten nothin' but potatoes for weeks . . . even had rickets when I was a baby. . . . Guess my mother couldn't board me out with anybody better. But we had chicken almost every Sunday when I stayed at my aunt's. My cousins and I got so we called it the 'gospel bird' . . . thought we made it up for a long time but lots of colored people call it that."

"I 'member when this country was the greatest in the world," she said. "We were first in everything . . . the first! Now the Russians are threat'n, Red China's threat'n, those black heathen savages ov'ver in Africa . . . we just use'ta be the greatest." She continued to shake her head in bewilderment.

The car stopped and the conductor peered from behind his seat. "Hey, Grace, this is Wilshire. Hey, Grace, here's your stop," he yelled above the beat of the twangy blues.

With a heave, the woman lifted her bulk and looked down at me. "You don' wan' ta marry mah girl, do you?"

"Nawh, lady. Nawh. I don't even know her."

"I use'ta want ta do things," she said. "Do things for that rotten girl of mine so she could get some of the things I didn't get. I don' know what went wrong."

"C'mon, Gracie, honey. You know I got a schedule."

"We use'ta be way ahead . . . so far ahead. Mah folks settled this country, walked across'd it an' ev'rything. . . . We killed the Indians for this place." The old woman shook her head and shuffled to the exit. "Where did we go wrong? Where . . .?"

When she stepped from the treadle the doors hissed shut and the car lurched forward to the strumming of a funky guitar.

"Ole Gracie's been riding with me for over five years now," the conductor yelled back at me. "Her daughter took off with a colored pimp from Chicago an' Gracie's been outta it ever since."

That evening at Len's had ended sourly. Like a young, spoiled apple its bitter tang stayed with me afterwards.

More people came. Ernest's plump girl. And some guys. Rick arrived wrinkling his nose and forehead, fussing loudly: "Brother Len

46

and his whiteman's culture." By then the promise of a new party lilted in the air with the cigarette smoke and strands of jazz. Soon Mona entered alone and joined me, her classy little legs bound by the straps of sandals and a pleated skirt above that showed her knees. And Rick became more contemptuous of the group's drinking. Also the jazz which played. His slurs annoyed me because I had contributed almost half the money for the beer and wine, and then he opened Len's refrigerator and finding the ham, gave a lecture to us all about the evils of pork consumption.

"Pork is filthy! . . . A product of the depraved devil's culture!"

"Wow, is he far out," Mona said. "I'd give it up without mah po'k chops," she drawled.

"Shusss, baby, let's hear what he's got to say."

She put a small cool palm into mine and hugged me to stifle a laugh; and I thought when I discovered her jasmine perfume: *This is going to be your girl, Stevie Benson, this is going to be your girl, you lucky fuck.*

Lou began cursing Rick but Len quieted her and she stood beside the kitchen doorway and blinked back tears, bobbing her head and tapping a long narrow shoe on the grass rug.

Many in the room didn't take Rick seriously, not even Ernest, who was ordinarily his ally, for the drinks had had their time, and I found Mona drawing closer to me after I made a couple of adolescent wisecracks which Rick turned aside with witty jabs.

After the pork lesson Rick brought up the incident of Ernest and me at the liquor store.

"It wasn't nothin'," Ernest said too modestly as Rick distorted how the man threatened us with the gun.

Rick went on a tirade against Jews. Two fellows who I had not seen before that night but who had entered with a jug of wine suggested we all go back and get the storekeeper.

"You shouldn't talk like that!" Rick screamed. *"Can't you ever quit being savage and not showing forethought?"*

"Look, Rick, who the hell you callin' a savage?" the big one asked.

"But I didn't call you a savage, *brother,* only that if you went

47

down there and caused a commotion it would make you *seem* to act like a savage."

The man had a flat nose and his well-dressed form seemed about to swell out of his suit and shirt. "That's not what you said at first, Rick." The big man shook his head and glowered. "Nawh nawh . . . I heard what you said. Don't come with that jive ta me."

"Brother," the big man's companion said to Rick. "Brother, you're beginning to sound like one of those ineffectual black intellectuals."

"You just don't *understand!*" Rick nearly wept. "Jews are the jackals of the slums. . . . The blood-sucking Jew has got to go before the black man can achieve dignity for himself . . . but it has to be done without violence. . . . Violence is wasteful and unnecessary, brothers."

"Ahhh, sheet . . ." Lou said.

"Are you going back?" Mona asked me.

"No."

She squeezed my hand tighter.

"Well, I don't know 'bout all that intellectual jive, Rick," the large man said. "But I think we should at least walk down the corner and ask 'Charles' why he jumped bad with Ernest and his partner." He had scar tissue ridging his brows, and the drinks had made his eyes beady.

"But, brother," his smaller friend pleaded to Rick and the group, "this sittin' 'round talkin' ain't goin' do nothin'. We should take proper action now and go and kick whitey's nose off."

"Yeah, let's go an' stomp that Jew mahthafukker," Ernest joined in, his drunken voice raspy. His girl clutched his arm and spoke low to him.

"Yeah, Tony, we're with you," someone said to the smaller of the pair.

"We'll teach him not ta call black men boys anymo'," another voice said.

"But violence isn't the way, brothers," Rick shouted. "The man didn't attack none of us. We're not a mob. Be intelligent for once!" Rick watched the African from the side of his eyes and made motions

48

with his hands and body as if he were on stage. The African sat silently and looked out at everyone.

"Listen to Martin Luther King," someone retorted.

"Jest sounds like another handkerchief hea' nigger ta me," a voice answered.

The youth called Tony, who accompanied the large man, spoke and gestured almost exactly like Rick. He looked like a slightly larger imitation. While Rick debated against another confrontation with the liquor store owner, the boy prodded the crowd and suggested they go out into the streets for vengeance.

Both Rick and the youth condemned the store owner in derogatory terms and took cues from each other when to slip in a blow about the man's ancestry, mentality and manhood. It was certain after the first moments, as the large man cooled off, that no one there that evening would leave and search out the liquor store proprietor unless they wished him to sell them some of his stock.

"You all shouldn't be talking like that," Mona argued after they made more statements about the Jew. "If the man at the store got into an argument with you," she said, "it wasn't because he's Jewish. Listen to all of you arguing now; it doesn't mean anything to you."

"You don't understand, sister," Rick began.

"That's right." Len spoke for the first time since Rick's pork speech. "It's all the whites who are to blame, but we have to deal with the Jew each and every day. They rob the members of the ghetto in their 'mama 'n' papa' stores day in and day out." Len spoke very precisely, showing up most of the others, who had lapsed into dialect.

"You should stop that shit, Lenard," Lou taunted. "After all the talk I hear from you 'bout suckin' round all those little skinny-assed Jew bitches at school . . . you better not say another word. . . ."

"Lou, you just don't understand . . ."

I had never heard negroes talk that way about Jews. Since my first schooldays I had assumed the Jew and the negro were the best of friends. Certainly, I had met plenty negroes who repeated Jewish jokes that they had learned from their white Protestant and Catholic

49

employers, fellow workers and friends, but this group at Len's had an entire black anti-Semitic tenet. There was no accident of chance meeting among a few there who had similar antagonisms, and even those few who disagreed, except for Mona, came out with the same jargon and argued with the exact rationale: that Jews were one of the negroes' worst afflictions. Even we who objected did it so weakly that we became doubtful of our positions at last. I sided with Mona and attempted to use logical arguments, but their emotional and illogical replies and taunts soon had us contradicting ourselves. The arguments of Rick and most of his crowd that night must have been worked out by blacks, for the word "white" was often interchanged with "Jew."

Through palm-lined streets my heels scurried after the ten-minute pace from the trolley stop. With the moonlight casting suspicious shadows, I chased my own quietly as I neared home, praying no patrol car intercepted me before I reached my house. I thought of the nights I had been halted by the L.A. cops in that no man's land for black men and was questioned as to why I was in that neighborhood at night. I shivered, from the shock of their steely examining fingers exploring me, and I remembered the minutes of sweating, crouching waits the times they ran their "makes" on me, and of the several nights I had ridden downtown in the back seats of their black and white cruisers, my hands manacled behind me. And I dreamed of the day when I would kill them all.

After the group took sides, most of us began drinking too fast, knowing the evening's loss, hoping to reclaim our spirits, which had dropped down hourly in a tight gyre. Mona and I left Len's with Rick's denunciations and pleas ringing out into the courtyard, flitting back from the stucco walls and cement surfaces like bats. Lou said good night and sorry, and I shook Len's hand, promising to return shortly. The windows in the other apartments in the unit were as black and vacant as the alley we passed through to the street, but across the court some were lighted, and a toilet flushed and for a

50

moment a record machine started to tumble old brash boogie out into the dark, until somebody jerked the needle off, scratching the record to shriek. Mona took my arm and I smelled her wet woman smell from being out late and being emotional too long after her bath, yet it gave me sensuous memories, and I wanted to get so close to her that my senses would bore into her odors and flavors and textures.

As we passed the liquor store we paused at the corner for the light, and watched the girl in pink capris drinking a red soda, not seriously but as a thing given her with her not knowing its full value or meaning. She and the bald man leaned at the far end of the counter next to the window. Her pink tongue played in the bottle opening, spitting air into the container and plugging the liquid in the end, then she would jerk the bottle down, swishing the last of the beverage around in the bottom, though leaving her tongue tip out, pointing red and moist at the owner. He leaned over the counter, the neon Coke signs flashing on his head.

In the empty store, the negro clerk closed and locked doors and emptied trash and swept the floor.

"I'm separated from my husband," Mona said as we neared her house.

"Has it been long?"

"Seven months . . . He still can't believe it's all over. He comes over a lot."

"Have you thought about moving?"

"I don't know," she muttered. "I just can't seem to refuse him. I want him as bad as he wants me, I guess, but it just won't work between us."

We walked through the night streets, the lawns bordering our steps with dried, weed-stuffed breasts, the streets at our sides deserted except for leaf-filled gutters. We brooded in private, and at her door I kissed her and filled my mouth and nostrils with her before she pushed me away.

"Don't think it's love with me, Steve."

51

"I'm afraid of love."

"It's because we can't."

"Give it time," I whispered as the first gust of the breezes between night and dawn groveled over the mountains, slinking down into the L.A. basin, shoving fog before them.

"Good night, friend," she said, kissing me quickly.

"See you tomorrow? Okay?"

And I went off across the lawn, through fog, not knowing if I would remember her face later that day when I was to meet her.

The bus pulled in almost at dawn. It had been a long trip for the man, a trip extending across the country, meandering back through his past and crisscrossing a life style that he had dropped through disuse and age. Where he started out he knew had been once called home, a place he had begun from many times before, but this time it no longer seemed as home, a place of warmth and security, a memory to be forgotten, to be placed outside of his mind, for he knew he would never return there.

This place, the place the bus had come to, was different and he had just landed with fifty cents in his pocket.

A bus ride across country is a horrible experience, he thought. Slow. Torturous. Grinding. Cruel.

He had begun at New York, then first headed south along the coast, visiting old friends and relatives and drifting from one place to another. And when he had gotten near the Deep South he had turned back northward and continued as far as Boston, where he laid over and became acquainted with the city briefly. But growing tired of the aimlessness of not settling in the East, where so many of his starts had become dead ends, he decided upon the West and headed first back to New York and then outward across the middle country he had never seen before.

His money had been short. Hardly more than enough for his bus ticket and a week or two of living money after he landed, but he was strong and knew that he would survive under almost any conditions, for he had survived up to that moment, under the duress of living in an urban desert and of being a loner and a traveler after whatever he sought.

The memory of the past, of his wasted years from where he came, from his previous trips searching for that something he sensed but hadn't found, had left him open to accept that there might not be anything to discover on this shore, like the bleakness, the lost and hurt of the shore he had just left, or the shores he had touched previously in Europe, in Africa, in the West Indies and in South America. Shores that promised life—life in terms of adventure and hope; life in terms of promises fulfilled and dreams realized. Though he never found the wealth of the land. Not in its reserves of minerals or produce, not in its people and cities. Not in the bodies of its women.

And so he stepped now upon this new shore, a last shore for him for many years, and he headed toward light. The bus station was near empty this time of day and he kept on through, only stopping to check his one heavy suitcase and small travel bag, for bus stations are the same, he knew, so it was for him to scout the city and find newer things before he returned for his belongings.

He scouted along Main Street, perceiving the area he was in, an area not too unlike the Boweries across the land in most metropolitan districts. A sign flashed COME TO JESUS and he knew where he would eat that morning. The men were lined up waiting to enter and he took his place in the line, silently, with hardly anyone noticing him. A drifter is a drifter, black or white, and even if he wasn't soaked with cheap wine anybody could see that he was down and out.

The door up ahead of the men cracked and the line stumbled forward, then halted, and then the men waited again. A pint of sherry was passed. He waved it by. Someone went past him; he did not see who, for his eyes were upon his shoes, and he was handed a grimy card. He looked at it in the light of the coming day. "If you want work come to . . ." The card gave an address and directions. He pocketed it before the line moved again and he entered the cool dimness inside to drink his watery coffee and mouth gluelike oatmeal.

Later he passed down the street, now filling with bodies bustling to work or to hustles which required the light of day. He belched. Coffee sometimes did that to him when it was cheaply made. A sign read DONORS WANTED. He turned inside.

I felt bad about taking it the first time. Though it was nice, so much better than I had imagined. The firmness of her box surprised me. She was so drunk she couldn't handle the strength of my attack, so I had had my way with her like I wanted.

I had been away several years. To the service, to prison, to sea again, and back to the home town. She had been on wine, I knew, even before I left. Once I visited her after we had gotten out of school together. I was back from some trip of a year or two and ran into her on the avenue. She invited me to her place and I went. She was looking much older, worn. In school, somewhere among my dreams, she had been my heart's desire, Delores. Black, fine, with pearly pearly white teeth and a shape that burst my heart almost since she wouldn't give me any but told me many times that she loved me.

And I went to her dirty apartment, drank some wine and laughed with her. She loaned me some money; her welfare check was cashed before picking up the wine. We listened to her record player and whispered of the old times until her kid woke up and some of her drinking buddies came by, so I split.

Passing through home base a couple of years later I met her again, in some bar. She was still drinking wine; two of her once pearly teeth were missing from the front lower half of her mouth.

"Some motherfucker beat my ass," she said as I ordered her a double. "You still my play boyfriend, Chuckie?" she asked.

"Always," I said.

She kissed me on the cheek and struggled to the ladies' room.

"I got two kids now," she said when she returned. "Cute little motherfuckers. . . . Both got different daddies and the welfare people wants me to turn them in."

"That's too bad," I said.

"I ain't even got no man now," she said and drained her glass.

Two more drinks and she was almost too drunk to walk. The bartender winked at me, and I paid the bill, led her out to my car and drove to a dark side street I knew of, took off her black panties and used her until dawn.

The only thing she said was when I first entered her: "You're a sonnabitch."

She stumbled up her front stoop later, me watching that she got into the house okay, and she didn't look back, only headed for home, while my eyes misted up thinking of my beautiful, lovely, black black Delores of the flashy smile from the time that I didn't believe in from then on.

And the last time I met her I had returned to one of my many schools under the GI Bill and had been there for a year or so. I ran into her on South Street.

She didn't recognize me at first. By the second drink she had put my face together. So she smiled because she knew we were friends.

I took her to my apartment, gave her a beer and undressed her. She resisted a little but just before my second orgasm she kissed my face and asked me why hadn't I stayed nearby her, before, when we were innocents and had been play man and woman?

She was snoring in my bedroom when I left her and got a fresh beer, and I was looking at a monster movie on the late late show by the time my roommate came in.

He had been to the library, he said, studying for an exam in sociology or something like that which I didn't understand.

"Who's in your bed?" he asked.

"Something I found," I said.

"Sharing?" he asked.

"If you take my sheets with yours tomorrow when you go to the laundromat."

He put his books in his room, went in the bathroom to get some rubbers and came out and went to the icebox.

"Ready for a fresh one?" he asked.

"Yeah."

He handed me my beer on his way into my room and shut the door. Sweet sweet Delores cried out once:

"Please no!"

Then all behind the door was silent.

I popped the top on my brew and watched Dracula fly through a window.

Forty-five minutes later he walked out with his blood money. Four brand-new, bank-fresh one-dollar bills were tucked safely inside his slim wallet.

He didn't care that prices out here were the lowest in the country for selling blood. A bit lower. But not so he would mind. He had sold his blood regularly in other cities. And used the money to pay his room rent or buy meals or even to go to the movies.

He knew his blood was still good, good for something. And he smiled knowing that he was worth something.

It was midafternoon before he reached the other end of town and found the address that was on the card. He looked across the lawn to the house, tucked behind hedges with a long low roof sloping over the porch. The front doorbell rang silently within the depths of the sprawling house. He waited, practicing a trick he had learned as a door-to-door salesman. Standing well away from the door with his body half-turned toward the street, looking absent-mindedly sideways so his full face wouldn't be seen. The door cracked and a voice said, "What can I do for you?"

He turned and handed the old black woman the card.

"The reverend ain't in. Come back tonight."

"I thought you wanted me to work," he said.

"Come back late tonight," the woman said behind the screen door. "He'll be in then."

The man moved away.

"And come 'round the back nex' time, ya hear?"

The door slammed.

The first woman I really raped was white. I mean really raped. Of course I had tried with most of my play girls during my growing up time but they had too much tomboy in them or their brothers would exact awful punishment from me so these token attempts didn't pan out until I was older and wilier. But the summer night I first really scored was like many other summer nights back then on the corner. We were boozing port wine this time. Some of my partners: Bam'a lam, Coozie, Foots and Nate. Most of the Snakes—that's who we were, the Sepia Serpents, Snakes for short—were off somewhere and we were doing what we did every summer night. Goin' down with what change we had or could hustle and gittin' down with a jug. Somewhere along the line, after a couple of jugs had been wasted, Lump Lump from down on Thompson came up on the corner. Now Lump Lump is okay, ya know, but bein' that he from down the way and not from up the way we cool on his case.

"Lump Lump . . . you crazy mahthafukker . . ." Coozie said. "What's happenin', nigger?"

Coozie's the actor among us. A sucker never knows where he's comin' from until ole Cooz moves on him.

Lump Lump, being forever a supercooly himself, said, "Dig, niggers, if you want to git you some white pussy just follow me."

"No shit!" Bam said.

"Really," my man Lump replied.

And juiced as we was we didn't ask too many more questions but followed ole Lump, good though jive nigger that he was.

Just a block away, down in an abandoned basement, just like Lump had said, was this old drunken white woman. It was dark down there, since there wasn't nothin' but candles, but she was white and drunk and had her dress above her hips and no drawers showin', seein' that Cisco from over on Camac was humpin' for all his skinny black ass was worth. There were other guys down there but I didn't notice them too tough, just waited my turn at the meat and then worked out.

"Uuuhhhggg . . ." I moaned. And somebody was tapping me on the shoulder saying it was their chance. While I had her she kept muttering and saying, "God, won't it ever stop." And I rolled off and got myself together and split.

Half an hour later I was sittin' up in the Heat Wave Café when Jellyman, the number man, passed through and stopped.

"I heard about you dumb young niggers," he said to me.

"Who, me?" I said.

"Stop tryin' to be so goddamn smart, little nigger! Look at the mud on your shoes and the shit on the front of your pants. If I was a cop I could get you thirty to life, little wise pussy-hungry nigger."

"Thanks, Jellyman. . . . If there's anything I can . . ."

"Shutup! . . . and get your ass out of here," he said.

It was near midnight when he went through the gate and followed the cement path to the back of the rambling house. A dim light showed the back screen door. The man was careful not to stray off the path and step onto the well-clipped grass; and he placed his feet down gently so as not to awaken any sleeping dogs, for he thought that such a wealthy-looking establishment must be provided with some kind of security measures. Behind the house the land opened out into a large yard; the moon did not outline its full depth or dimensions but the man knew by various shapes and shadows that there were garage and shedlike buildings on the property as well as the house he now stood at the back door of. A light shone secretly from within one of the low structures off the yard.

He stepped up to the back door and knocked softly. "A sucker's knock," he muttered to himself. But there was sound somewhere inside the house, then a light went on and a large shape was at the door.

"Yes," a male voice said.

"I got a card . . ." the man began.

58

"Yes, you're the one. Wait . . . I'll be right with you."

The figure disappeared for a moment, and it came back holding a flashlight.

"Follow me," it said.

Further back in the yard, behind foliage, was the source of the light, a small barn like building where inside burned a kerosene lamp showing several beds with occupants reading or playing checkers.

"Good evening, Reverend," a white-haired man said.

"Evening, Ted," the man's guide said. "Now I told you about that light burning all night. You want to fall asleep and catch the place on fire and burn you all up. What would the state say about that now? Come now, turn it out and be good fellas and go to sleep now."

He pointed to a couch. "You can sleep there, young man."

Before he left he asked the white-haired man, "How's Jeff doin'?"

"Fine, Reverend. He's 'sleep."

"And Annie?"

"Just fine, Reverend."

The light went off and the pudgy man was gone and the new man lay down on the unmade couch, his nostrils stinging from the old urine smell, the disinfectant and the scent of age and death as he closed his eyes to fall asleep.

"Hey, mister," he heard from somewhere in the room. "Hey, you," a female voice said. "You got any smokes?"

"Nawh," the stranger said. "They cost more than I can afford."

Then all was black and silent and he did not know anything more until the sun rose.

I guess the first Black Nationalist I knew was my mother. Not that she was a real doctrinaire nationalist like a Garveyite or a follower of Elijah Muhammad, but she believed in art and culture in a genteel sort of colored way and believed that colored folks, as she would say, could be artistic too. She must have read W. E. B. Du Bois though I've never asked her. But she was a great reader and once a chorus girl and childhood friend to Marian Anderson, but in later years disliked Marian for being so dicty and hiring white servants and

59

such. But my mother took me to the church and community center cultural events and programs, and there I saw black people singing and playing instruments and reading poetry that put me to sleep. And she would somehow put things in a colored-folks context no matter if they were subjects like the Second World War, Joe Louis, school integration, Jackie Robinson or FDR. But more important, I guess, she stressed that I become an accomplished reader, which I am still working at in my lackadaisical style.

He didn't sleep soundly. All night he sensed movement inside the small building and several times mutters nearly woke him from his light sleep but his breathing relaxed and his brain did not call him through the threshold of slumber, but his senses found the sounds seeming to come from one of the beds against the far wall.

At dawn someone entered the building and a rooster crowed somewhere out in the dimness. He opened his eyes and saw a cobwebbed ceiling and the dim illumination showed him that no one moved inside the room but him. He pulled on his shoes and wiped sleep from his eyes. Soon, at the back door of the house, he knocked and the old woman appeared.

"Come in," she said. "The reverend is out this morning but he left your instructions."

She showed him a small toilet off the back porch where he washed and relieved himself. Upon entering the kitchen he was shown a bowl of oatmeal and poured a cup of coffee. It was the best coffee that he had drunk in months, he thought. After breakfast he was given his duties. To mop the downstairs of the large house, which he found to be a home for old black people, then to clean the yard and clip the hedge or mow the lawn or do whatever the taciturn old woman demanded.

By early afternoon he was through with his duties.

"Is there anything else?" he asked the woman.

"Nawh, not till the reverend comes and tells you somethin'. You ain't supposed to get no lunch but dinner will be ready this evenin'."

He went downtown and got his bags. It wasn't hard to figure out the bus routes. There were so few of them on this end of town that he walked to the larger uptown-downtown streets and waited, then made connections or walked across.

When he returned with his bags the old woman wasn't in sight. He placed his bags inside the back porch, to the side of the door, and not knowing whether to go back to the little house where he had slept, but knowing it wasn't a wholesome place in smell and appearance, he walked about the neighborhood.

This part of the city was well taken care of by its almost completely black residents. The lawns were clipped uniformly. And sprinklers spewed water in rainbow swirls about the feet of the palms. Not many people were seen, only the stark emptiness of their curtained windows, except for an occasional child or teen-ager who rode a lonely bike or bounced a ball. The man later learned that the residents of this black island of affluence came in from their jobs at evening and entered their homes and remained in front of their televisions until past midnight and then went to bed, to appear just past dawn driving away to their employment, unless they had already left sometime in the night to other jobs. On the weekends these workers were seen in comparatively large numbers washing their late-model cars or burning meat over outdoor grills. They drank whiskey and some beer, name brands certainly, and strove to enjoy their good lives desperately, so desperately that the soft hysteria lurking behind their eyes could only be shielded by their sunglasses.

The sun burned down, uncompromising, and the wide streets threw back shimmers of heat in their emptiness. The man walked, coming finally out to larger boulevards and avenues where the machines of commerce belched and rolled, intimidating the varied smaller autos to keep out of their way. A sign across a road showed TACOS. He had never had one. The words looked unfamiliar but he recalled the word from the back of his mind, though he had never tasted or experienced this thing, a taco.

There was a brown-skinned Mexican-looking girl working alone in the small stand.

"Whatta ya have?" she asked.

"A take-co, please."

"You want a *taco?*"

"Yeah, a taco."

She turned, did some swift exercises and turned back soon with what he ordered.

Shoving it on the counter, she asked, "Where you from?"

"The East."

"Oh. . . . Like it here?"

"Don't know yet," he said.

"Want anything to drink?"

"Yeah, give me a Coke."

He ate his taco, drank his Coke and watched the traffic go by. The girl had the radio turned to a rock-'n'-roll station and she occasionally popped her fingers and bobbed her head.

"How did you know I wasn't from around here?" he asked her.

She smiled and shrugged her shoulders. After a while he left.

Before he had disappeared down the street the girl said to the beat of the blues, "Because you're so dumb, brother."

I knew about politics from an early age. I didn't know what politics was but I knew about politics. Like when my cousins and I picked up on the slogan "Fooey on Dewey" and were laughed at and joked with by our family members who were older than us. They agreed with our childish jingle about sentiments they did not express. Roosevelt was my mother's and aunts' savior. And I knew about the campaign workers who came through whatever neighborhood we lived in then, workers from all the parties, and how when the communists came my mother wouldn't open the door because she did piecework in a government plant, but my stepfather, who read a lot and had been in the war, would go out and talk with the sincere-looking men and women in extended conversational raps, to the distress of our neighbors, newly from the South, though my mother took secret pride in my stepfather's daring. And I saw how the local ward politicians got out the vote on election days, which were school holidays as well, and the liquor stores were closed. Later, when I was older and in the white-lightning whiskey business, election days became some of my most profitable business days. But when I was a child I saw the committeemen come with one-, two- and five-dollar bills in their tight fists, to get out the vote. And for some of my neighbors, only a swig out of a bottle of "good stuff" was enough to get them to walk up the block to someone's house, converted for this great occasion into a democratic institution, a polling place, and pull whatever lever they had been guided to. But neither my mother nor my stepfather bothered to vote. They were of the new breed, I guess. So they never voted for anything I know of, anyway, but worked hard each day for the things they wanted and left voting to the innocents and idealists. People would ask them why they didn't do more about the conditions of the nation and get out there and pull that lever but they only looked away, or my stepfather would go into strange stories of what he saw when he went off to fight for his country. They never voted; *never* did, not in that period of their lives, at least. Not for the party of Lincoln. Or for FDR, who they said had led the country out of depression over the bodies of millions through creation of the war. They read too much, you see. And would not even cast their lots with the silly socialists or the crazy communists who they said promised to save the world for we workers, black that we were, yet not understanding the world we blacks lived in. But I never could understand how these beliefs, this huge faith, politics, that pressed men into its service on a do-or-die basis, had anything to do with me. For I learned early that I was black. And being black I was outside of systems made by white men for the place and people I lived among, wherever that was. Things are supposed to be changing, I hear. But I would be very surprised if the Second Coming overtook me in this life and country. At least I'll never be caught attempting to vote it in on a machine ticket.

He knew she had seen him watching her. Or he wished she had. By the extra swing she put in her hips. By her back-of-the-hand nose-wipe and frowning at the boogie that tickled the back of her nose. By the extra popping of her gum as she crossed the street and came up on the curb behind him.

He liked dark girls, but she was light, almost albino, and was a superbad street mama.

"Hey, girl, how's your baby?" she said.

He saw her join a dark girl in pink leotards covered by bright hot pants. They walked almost abreast of him, smiling, rolling their big young behinds and popping their gum.

"Butchie's fine, honey," the girl said. "How's yours?"

"He's so bad. My mother took him out to the park. I'm sure glad she did. Mom and me smoked some boss reefer, girl. And I got so high I couldn't deal with the little bastard. Then Mom took the little mahthafukker to the park, girl."

The girls went into a candy store on their block and the man kept walking. He knew he would see her the next time he walked on that side of the street.

Bennie and I had this real estate company. Seems funny now but we really had these broken-down buildings. We met in the post office. Both of us were working killing hours, sometimes twelve, sixteen hours a night, and going to school too under the GI Bill, and we both had hustles on the side. Bennie cut a tonk game over on the west side of town and I sold some white lightning—you know, cooked corn whiskey—at a low-lights joint up around my old neighborhood. I had a big family by then, so I had to keep my behind in gear, and Bennie was just greedy.

We began talking money, future, business, etc., while tossing mail. And after a few months we had our company, Ben & Benson, Inc. I was going to business school so could keep some light books and Bennie was from one of those big southern colored families and grew up around undertaker/grocery/dentist/schoolteacher/doctor/business and allied activities, so could wheel and deal with a country flourish. We saved our money, put in more killing hours at our various jobs and schemes, and in several more months we had our first deposit.

After looking around a bit we found a run-down tenement that we could pay down on. We found a flashy/slick Jewish real estate family —a father, wife and platinum daughter—who would have sold us a cemetery if we had enough to make the first payment. And the properties we invested in weren't too far from graveyard city at that. The bank didn't like our being so young, with me just turning twenty-one but able then to sign contracts, but money talks and with our shyster real estate agents we walked with the deeds.

In eighteen months we had two more buildings and were foolishly pushing for more. I guess we thought that quantity could make up for absence of any redeeming values. It's hard to think of it now for me; it's so painful. We had to borrow to make the notes and the fuel bills were always behind. The properties were in such bad shape. Talk about slumlords—we made ourselves actually slum slaves to those death traps, chasing the dynamic dollar, caricaturing the American dream.

I got my cousin Elvin to do some painting, plumbing and plastering, but we could hardly even afford his minimal expenses. For every spare penny had to go into the buildings.

My family suffered for my ambition. My wife was always going home to her mother. As soon as I went and got her and brought her back to our house I would have to be off to work or school or to see about the business, and by then most of my income was going to the business, not my home. And the only thing my ole lady could see and understand of my hyperactivity was that we were living worse and not hiding our personal misery.

Whenever I would go to my mother-in-law's place to collect my wife and children, my wife's mother would say, "Are you crazy, man? You're too far into this thing. Look at your family. They can't take this kind of stuff. Get out. It's not paying. Get out!"

But how could I explain to her that I had sunk all my savings into those ghetto holes, all the money I had saved in the service and going to sea, from days on end and sleepless nights of poker, from smuggling contraband in the ports my ships touched in Europe, Africa, the West Indies and South America. How could I describe to her all the hours of mind-deadening labor I had done on all the jobs I had worked the past three years to achieve the success of being a man of property.

How could I tell *anyone* that I had nearly killed to get some of the money and these blemishes on my soul could only be removed through work and study, and finally, when I could afford to, sometime in the near future, through service to the people. But even then there was more I could not admit to myself, as my dreams dissolved like wet plaster, than to anyone else, and who could understand a word I spoke or any single feeling that I had?

When my wife would appear from the interior of the protective confines of my in-laws' household we would quarrel briefly, then I would help her pack for the last time, of course, to return to our home.

But then I almost immediately had to leave her after our welcome-home lovemaking and storm out to conquer the world.

My partner, Bennie, was a vulgar, ruthless and stingy small-town talent, and gradually I grew not to trust or like him. And he had the traditional southern dislike for northern street niggers. Not that either of us had much to worry about in terms of each other ripping the other off. The real estate agents and the bank had done such a good job there wasn't anything in the pot left to cop; we could only turn out our pockets and keep shelling out to forestall foreclosure. A real estate agency handled rent collections except for an exception or two which I'll get to in a minute.

And I began to change visibly. I didn't go to my old haunts. I dressed conservatively, at least to my way of thinking then. Sports jackets. Slacks. Lavender shirts with orchid-colored ties. Stingy-brimmed Dobbs "sky pieces." Something called the Bold Look was in then. I even took to carrying a briefcase, for I was studying for my real estate salesman's license.

And I tried to change my speech. Began using the big words that I heard in school and encountered in reading, and more often than not I mispronounced them. Even when I would stop into a bar on the avenue and meet some of the old dudes from down the way I would throw my new vocabulary on them. Hardly anyone said anything to me, though eyebrows were raised; mostly, I guess, they remembered that just a couple of years before that I would knock most monkeys out for batting their eyes at me, but my new credit-bought clothes didn't hide my heart. Oh, I would come on like "Good afternoon, gentlemen. Would you care to partake of spirits and endeavor to render a discourse concerning the exceptional circumstances of our existential beings existing *a priori* to this philosophical incident?" Wow, talk about going corny. I could hardly stand myself most of the time. But I was out to make it in the big world, and I knew there was some kind of game to be learned and played. And I had to learn it. So I was getting my education, all right. Though my style was turning off my old crowd and had me moving into some life patterns that developed out of my oversized head, rather than those I found in my surroundings and experience.

I even acquired a subscription to the *Wall Street Journal* and read it on the subway going to work at the post office. When Bennie and I could get places next to each other to throw mail, we would discuss stock prices, although neither of us owned any shares, and our next projected real estate acquisitions, even while part of our pay and hustling money was drained off to meet our mortgages and fuel expenses.

I would have voted Republican, if I'd had the chance or taken the time to register. They were the party of the rich, right? I shudder now at my mental condition then, but for almost three years I was off on a success American style trip, and that's more than enough to damage any black's brain.

But things weren't too successful for me at my household.

He came in just past dusk. Dimly a light shone from the house, and following the path to the back, he knocked at the door and saw a shadow. The middle-aged pudgy brown man that he met the night before came to the door. He switched a light on.

"Hello there, young fellow," the man said.

"Yeah . . . I was here . . ."

"Yes, you're the young man who is helping us out. Come in," he said, holding open the door. "Have you had dinner?"

"Nawh, sir."

"Well, just come in then. The cook must have left something."

The older man fixed him cold cuts and chatted. The stranger hungrily scarfed his food while the older man told him that his name was Parsons, Reverend Parsons, and that he owned the house and kept it to help the sick and aged. "The state and social security pays the bills, of course." Somewhere in the house a television broadcast the news.

"Have you any family, son?" Reverend Parsons asked.

"Some, but they all back east."

"Then why are you all the way out here, young fellow?"

"I heard that schools are less expensive out here."

The reverend agreed with that, then he poured the young man some lemonade and patted his shoulder.

"Well, I'm glad that you like it here, son. You do like it here, don't you?"

"Oh, yes. Yes, I do."

"I sent out the word some time ago among the local missionaries to send me any young colored men who come through their houses. Of course they must appear to be only a victim of hard times or lost and strayed from the path of salvation. No drug addicts. No imbibers of the devil's grape. No, my son, only poor, homeless colored boys. Oh, how I do like young boys."

The reverend smacked his lips at this last statement and tied an apron about himself. The young man ate silently, watching Reverend Parsons busying himself about the kitchen. After the food was gone the reverend took the plate and set it in the sink.

"Your bags are in the broom closet," the reverend said. "Get them and I can take you over to the little house and introduce you."

He got his bags and followed the soft-bodied, heavy-set man out of the back door. They walked to the place where the man had slept the night before and the older man entered without knocking. In the light of more kerosene lamps the younger man saw that there were four people in the room, sitting in beds: the dark, white-haired man named Ted that he had seen the night before, a nearly bald, equally dark older man, and a skinny old man in long johns. The other person in the room was a plain-looking, work-worn black woman of undeterminable age.

Everyone greeted the reverend with a degree of deference, though the woman only looked absent-mindedly at him, as if she had forgotten his name and face.

"This young fellow will be staying with us for a while," said Reverend Parsons. "Please make him comfortable and put him at ease, won't you?" Then he cautioned them not to burn themselves to death and not to drink too much of their cheap wine and not to ruin their eyes playing that devil's game, cards.

"If our eyes ain't bad yet, Reverend, we goin'a see till you bury us," the old man named Jeff said.

They laughed at that.

"Annie," the reverend said to the woman. "Why don't you come with me? I got something for you to do. Good night, everybody. God bless you."

And he was gone, the woman following him through the door.

The skinny old man in long johns began wheezing, then spoke. "Ole rev . . . ole rev gonna keep gettin' his self a little bit of Annie till there ain't none left for you, Ted."

"Huhn . . . Ted couldn't get a hard-on if his ass depended on it," Jeff said. "All he could do is suck on ole Annie like a hound dawg suck on a bone . . . if'in Annie would heist up her leg fo him wit' her ignorant self."

In mock anger, Ted said, "At least I ken git outta bed an' go ta tha bathroom."

"Sheet . . . then why you bed so funky?" answered the old man in the soiled long johns.

"Sheet . . . you niggers better stop talkin' about Annie like ya do," said Jeff. "And you better stop treatin' her like ah dawg or she won't go to the store fo you on check day 'n' git you ya wine."

"Sheet . . . ole pappy Clark there would walk to the store for wine on his hands if he had ta," Ted said.

The three men kidded like that for a while, slapping their cards down on the table pulled between their beds, puffing at their pipes and Bull Durham, not bothering to notice the new man, until they began snuffing out their oil lamps, one by one.

"Night . . . sleep tight," one of them said to the younger man. "Don't let the bedbugs bite."

The man slept better that night, but he could distinguish the snores and breathing of the three old men he shared his quarters with, and he wondered why he hadn't noticed their pronounced sounds the night before. Later, toward dawn, his sleeping mind told him that he heard someone enter the little house and pass his sleeping place, muttering in his mother's voice, "Lord forgive me. . . . Lord God have mercy and forgive me."

I have wondered why some women I have raped have forever since believed that I disliked them. I never could understand this misunderstanding on their parts. How could they believe that? On the contrary, rarely is it the case that I dislike a source of my pleasure. And I would not knowingly take a woman's body that I did not desire, unless I was drunk, or terribly horny, or depressed, or it was very dark, or someone offered her to me and out of comradeship I couldn't refuse the generosity. . . . Or some other good reason along these lines. But for the most part I find the objects of my assaults very desirable. And some of my conquests understand this and treat my predatory acts as the compliments they are, once having recovered their composure after having been taken advantage of against their will, if it really was against their will. And some women I have raped have remained loyal lovemates to me for years, yes, years. For several, for more than half a dozen years. You see, after the initial taking was done they came to me, some after a few moments, some after several days, even years, and we started something long-lasting and permanent in a transitory sort of way; we became passionate and long-ranging long-distance lovers. Now, I'm a traveling man. I pass through a lot of places and I can usually be found some part of the year in one or two special places, so when I pass through one of my women's cities or they swing through mine, the word is passed and somehow we make it together to refresh and complete our lasting union. For they know that it is *they* I desire above all else, and most real women at least in some part of their lives wish to be wanted by a man more than anything else. And I humbly become a servant to this need. So our lovemaking lasts over decades, it crosses state and national boundaries, it surpasses the vows made to husbands and friends and families. For they know that at least I'll take them and appreciate them and do my best for their total satisfaction.

It seems strange to me that I become lumped with some type of freak or sex deviate who gets a charge out of hurting women because I take them sometimes against their will. But I use only the necessary degree of force to accomplish the act, none at all when none is needed. For when you embark upon an act as total as rape there is seldom a chance nor is it wise to turn back. I have engaged in fierce knuckle-bruising, biting, hair-tearing and throat-throttling battles with women to take possession of them and midway through my love-making they have become some of my most responsive and ardent bed partners. These are the types of women who will follow a man from state to state, from country to country, and live with him under any circumstances that he demands. For they belong to their ravishers wholly, for they have been stripped of everything but their pride, and as long as the man will love them and desire to touch their minds, bodies and souls they retain all that a man can allow one of his women, her pride. She is desired above all else, even life, and the proof of his faith in her is that he leaves his life in her keeping after

71

he walks out the door. For to commit rape is to commit oneself to one's own death, if the woman so wills it and if one allows her to live with this power to speak of it to the authorities, the official state protectors of female chastity and honor. So you live for that moment of life with her and gamble with death for her, and she understands the stakes and knows that she is your woman like no others can be, for out of her has been born another existence, more fragile than an infant's, that she alone can guarantee—*yours*. Truly, I am reluctant to rape any woman I could not love, if I willed myself to, and in whose hands I could not sense my life was safe, within limits, of course, though frankly, I would rape a snake if the opportunity presented its slinky self. After all, it's all relative to where one is, who one is with and what condition one is in.

So she is taken, for it is not for her to decide how her man is to use her. She is cherished as a separate and distinct part of a union, a union that binds man's universe together—man and woman. And there is no sexual pretense for her after her underclothes have been ripped away, her private parts exposed and the man enters her forcefully as if he were storming a divine citadel to take possession of a holy treasure that he alone knows the real value of.

After I take a woman's body and she has lost all fear that she'll be abused by me, then we can look into each other's eyes and discover everything, ourselves. For we are together then. Physically, in the *real* world, we are together: the lowest common denominator of our collective existence—man and woman—and this is all we ever truly wanted to be, if we will allow ourselves to release ourselves to this realization. For then body awareness falls away and we have our minds, our spirits, our sense of ourselves together as a unit, even while the individual parts may break and go separate ways until some accident of time in the future fuses us again. Our body falls away and we enter the psyche, for I do not desire dumb women, really dumb women, except as a release, and cannot tolerate a woman I cannot communicate with outside the physical plane, because some of my most profound learning has been in the company of women who are the moon to the sun of my manhood.

Reverend Parsons came for him after lunch. The younger man was doing yard work, trying to complete his duties satisfactorily and get some time to himself.

"Son . . . how're doin'?" the reverend asked him.

"Fine, sir," he answered, raking some palm fronds into a large burlap bag.

"Have you seen the entire grounds yet, young man?"

Still working, the yard worker shook his head, swept some foliage into the bag and said, "No, sir."

"Then come with me," the middle-aged man said. "I have something to show you."

The young man followed his employer away from the big house, past his small building, hidden by a clump of bushes, out of which came sounds of the old and invalid state-supported people he shared the premises with, and then behind a windbreak of trees to the very rear of the large lot. They followed a path that led through the trees to a sunny clearing. Here stood a small, single-story cottage, well painted and kept, with a goldfish pool in front of it and a small wooden bridge that had to be crossed before one could enter the little house. A birdbath stood to one side of the path, in the space of land fronting the house and bridge, and on the other side of the path a sundial told the time of day to anyone who could calculate by the ancient ornament.

"After you, young man," the reverend said, indicating the bridge.

The young man crossed it, stepping off upon the porch, and turned and waited for his chubby companion.

"Here we are," said the reverend, after he had crossed over the bridge and turned his key in the lock of the cottage's front door.

When they entered, the older man touched a light switch and low-keyed, tinted lights revealed the curtained room. It was done in velvety maroon and black—walls, ceiling, carpets, furniture and drapes.

"This is my study," the reverend said, smiling and waiting until the younger man's eyes drank in all of the splendor.

73

"You live well," the young man said.

"When I can," replied Reverend Parsons.

He moved to a black shellacked cabinet with fittings of white metal. From it he took a bottle and two glasses.

"I don't normally take spirits but this is a special occasion."

"It is?" said the young man.

"Yes," Reverend Parsons said. "We're celebrating your joining our household."

"Well, Reverend." The young man sighed. "I want to talk to you about that. . . . I'm only goin'a be here until I can get myself together. I didn't have any money when I got off the bus so I was ready to take almost anything to keep eating and get a place to stay. I . . . ."

"I understand. I understand, young man."

"See . . . I came out here . . ."

"Why don't we have our little drink first before you tell me *everything,*" the reverend said, smiling.

He handed the younger man one of the glasses, now filled with an amber liquid.

"No, thanks, sir. I have work to do. The cook told me that I was to finish the yard this afternoon."

"You mean Mrs. Parsons?"

"Oh, I'm sorry, Reverend Parsons," the young man stammered. "I didn't know she was your wife."

"Yes . . . yes . . . we don't talk much anymore . . . but we are married."

He showed the young man the couch.

"Come, why don't we sit down. No use standing in the middle of the floor like two idiots, is it?"

The younger man sat while the older turned on a stereo. Old-time negro spirituals played.

After the reverend was seated at the other end of the couch from his guest, he said, "Why don't you try your drink? It's cognac . . . good stuff." He drank his neat and poured himself another full glass.

"Don't you find religious music restful?" he asked.

The young man nodded his head and sipped his drink. The cognac was good stuff. He turned his head and looked at the room's paintings and tried to make out the book titles in the case across the room from his seat, and while his head was turned the reverend slid across the couch and tried to unfasten the young man's buttons on his trousers front. He stood up immediately, telling the older man, "Hey, mahthafukker! I don't play that kinda shit!"

After my marriage finally broke apart, I mean final, without recourse to reprieve or patchwork, my mind began fast disintegrating. And I hadn't expected that. I thought I was more stable than that, more together. But I found myself drinking progressively more and barflying again. I pawned all my suits, quit the post office, which was the best thing that I did that year, dropped out of school and moved out of my mother's flat, after a brutal, screaming tirade against her and all she had done for me, even bringing me into the world, to an apartment in one of my own buildings. The center had fallen out of that part of my life. And that's when I started daring real trouble to come to me, myself.

From somewhere, her mother certainly, my wife had heard that she would receive more money from the welfare than I could give her. My wife already had a boyfriend, someone who had been keeping her occupied the weeks and months and years that I was in the service, at sea or in jail. I could deal with that; I had lots of other women, didn't I? But she was my wife, I thought. And though I suspected who her nigger was I still was on the move to "make it" land, and I couldn't stop long enough to get hung up in trivialities and waste time. I was so cool I was stupid. So one day my ole lady had her new man move her and my kids out of our place, my mother watching mutely with tears in her eyes, while my children, who my mother had raised, gaily told her, "Good-bye, Granny. We're going bye-bye."

My wife moved from my mother's place to her mother's run-down joint over in the ghetto part of town we had moved away from. But my mother-in-law knew she could fix her place up better with a share of the welfare money that was coming.

I called over there and my father-in-law told me to stay away if I "knew what was good" for me. Now, he knew me, had watched me grow with his sons and daughters. He knew my nature, my temperament, so if I forced my way past that point there would be bloodshed.

I was at work when my wife made her move, but I knew it was coming so I didn't fight city hall. She had three more kids by me before I left that town for good; there's no need asking me how I know my children, but I would never consider taking her back after she had her boyfriend come to my mother's place when I was away at work and move her. Some things you can't allow a woman to get away with.

I drank more and became involved with a girl in the building that I moved to and several more in the neighborhood, and I began doing a light pimp thing with them, having them use my place above the bar in the basement that I used for an after-hours joint. But I stayed drunk or high on pills so much I didn't know what was happening for days. But they were good, mainly clean girls out to make some money to take care of themselves and their kids, and just breaking into the life, so they treated me good because my head was too messed up to be putting them in a heavy hustle game, and I ran a straight house that paid off the cops and kept violence outside. With me being in poor condition, the house limped along the best way it could, only because I had a good woman taking care of things. The girls took care of me and the house and kept me out of trouble the best way they knew how. That evil, self-destructive thing of mine was feeding inside of me, operating off of liquor and my pill diet, and I took to carrying a pistol which I pulled a couple of times to cool out the weekend crowd and word went around that a contract was out for me to move me out of my lucrative spot. But I was meeting the mortgage on the joint by then and I wasn't ready to share that. But more scary, I was relieving white cab drivers and johns of their wallets when I got drunk and mean and would wander the neighborhood, daring death to do his best.

Bennie kept his distance from me, not knowing this side of me, and

76

not wanting to get pulled into any beefs. He finally split town to settle his family's estate; his father was already dead, then his mother died and he and his brothers and sisters began fighting over the spoils. While he was down in Florida, where he came from, he met and married a girl, a mortician's daughter, and sent me her picture. She was so light I put the picture on the mantelpiece and the girls in the house would rank me by saying that I had gone and gotten me a white "hoe."

Sometimes my wife would come by when she got drunk. She was drinking heavily too, something she had never done before, and she would search me out, ask me to return to her for the sake of the children, then get furious when I said no after we had made love like we had done when we were teen-agers, and ridicule me by telling me that I didn't do it to her as good as her new men. I didn't mind too much. Somewhere inside I was numb and dying. And the stuff she was drinking made her breath and skin smell so bad that I could hardly bring myself to have anything to do with her, even for old times' sake. And she had some kind of female trouble by then and most of the time I couldn't do anything with her because of the odor and slime.

One morning I woke up, hearing the rats scuttling through the walls, after being drunk for I don't know how many days. The house was empty. None of the girls' voices could I hear. Nor was a black music soul station on. And a fresh smell of coffee wasn't in the house. I checked the mailbox. A letter with a bus ticket was in the mail from an old friend, Jack Bowen. The letter said he had heard from my mother that I wasn't doing too well since my marriage had broken up and if I wanted I could come down and sit on the farm for a while and relax.

I shook my head and laughed, not believing that things like that happened. I checked my pockets and found a couple of hundred dollars in my wallet. My main woman was taking care of things just like she always did.

I went back inside the house, cleaned up, changed into a fresh shirt and pants, left half of the money in my woman's drawer with the pistol, wrote her a note, put my key on top of it and walked out the door.

I've never been back and that was several lifetimes ago.

What unsettles me most with women is when they are aggressive. I never learned how to really handle that. After I make the first advance, sure, they can go for broke. But I want to make the first heavy hit. I'm not hung up, really. Some of my most lasting relationships with women were with those who wanted to get into the sex act as much as me or faster and didn't have any qualms about it. 'Cause if I don't make a broad on the first time go-round . . . well, there might not be any more go-rounds, unless I can get a chance to take some.

But there is a kind of woman I could never handle. Like I was walking up a street somewhere one day and this hoe was standin' on the corner. I've seen hoes before. I've even had one or two throwin' me some chump change. I'm not exactly dumb, ya know. And when I got abreast of her this funky whore said, "Lookin' for goodies, sport?"

I turned and replied, "I got six bitches that look so good that you can't even stand in their shadows, mamma!" You see, I was insulted that this woman would mistake me for a chump. And she said, "You may have six, papa, but mah thing's better!"

Our eyes really met for the first time, then I pulled away, not breaking my stride, and kept on round the corner.

You know, next day I went back and looked for her. She was gone, of course, and I've never found her. But I think of her sometimes and smile to myself and know that she'd make some man a mean bottom woman.

He had left Reverend Parsons standing in the middle of the gilded room called the "study." He hadn't hit the older man; no, he had more sense than that. Being a stranger in town with no money or contacts made him ripe for any accusation brought against him, he knew. He just walked out the door, slamming it, crossed the small bridge and walked up the path toward his cottage.

It wasn't that he was entirely naïve; he had suspected that Parsons was a faggot but he had to put on this show of injured indignation, he told himself, if he was going to stay there and keep the old man at a distance while he looked for a way out of the situation.

The old people were sunning themselves outside their house when he approached. Annie was shelling peas on the front step, humming one of the old-time spirituals that he had heard in the reverend's study.

He passed them and entered the door. Ted was inside, feebly relieving himself in a bucket.

"How ya doin', young fella?" he said.

"Okay, I guess."

"I see you're upset . . . so the rev's explained your job to you."

"What do you mean?" The young man tried to act angry.

"Ahhh . . . don't get riled up now, young fella. I'm from Nevada. And I don't talk city talk so good, ya understand? Bet you didn't know there was colored folks in Nevada, did ya? Nawh, I bet ya didn't. Well, mah family was there ever since the Injun wars back after the Reconstruction. . . ."

"Yeah . . . yeah . . . I heard about it," the young man said impatiently.

"But there's other things you ain't heard about, junior. So listen to an older man for a while. Now I can't pee so good, I know. But I know what I know from all these years that God allowed me to live on his land. . . . It was in the war, the First World War, where I caught the claps . . . bad, real bad. They didn't have no miracle drugs and things like that, not even over there in France then, so I ain't been able to piss so well these later years, but I seen the years go by."

"Look, old man . . . I don't feel so good."

"Why? Because the ole rev wanted to suck your thing some for you?"

The old man was sitting back on his bed again; he reached under his mattress and pulled out a pint of sherry. "Do you bother any with this stuff?" he asked.

The younger man shook his head solemnly.

"Then get a glass over there outta that box."

When his glass was gotten the old man filled it up.

"Now let's talk some, young man. . . . Now why and how did you get yourself in this predicament?"

"I wanted to go to school and I heard they were cheaper out here in the West."

"Well, that's the best reason that I found yet amongst you young shavers passing through here. Yeah, lots of youngsters come to California for one reason or another. Yeah, lots comes through here. The rev has his eyes out for young stuff like you. Now don't go blamin' him too much. He's a pretty nice guy in his own way. Lots of the people who run these kinds of places are lower than dawgs, nothing but scurvy critters. But ole rev feeds ya well and don't cheat you out of what's due you from the government or what your kids sends ya. C'mon, drink up. . . . Yeah, the rev's okay. . . . What's yours you get."

"But he tried to put his hand on me."

"Well, to him you're like a sweet little girl. . . . Now don't get upset. The rev's just funny like that. When his wife and him got married they were in the service of the Lord, ya know, some kind of missionaries, and they promised that they would never have anything to do with each other in a sexual way at their wedding. The rev told me all this his self, of course. Sure seems funny to me but they been together for over thirty years now and he tells me he's never even seen up under his wife's skirt."

"That's weird," the young man said.

"Maybe so, but it's the truth. . . . But the rev couldn't hold to his vows. He's got a couple of grown children who come to visit him every several years. His wife don't even seem to mind. She just goes off to pray for his soul and leaves him alone with his kids he had out of wedlock. And now that he likes young boys and fools around with Annie some she just acts like it's not happenin'."

"I don't know what to say," the young man said.

80

"Well, don't say nothin'," the old man said. "Just drink up . . . but if you want to find out about school you'd better get over to the high school over there on Vermont Avenue."

"But I'm too old to go to high school."

"Adult high school . . . evening school . . . Where you been all your life, son?"

"Oh, I thought . . ."

"Don't think so much. That's the trouble with you young fellas, you think nobody's got any sense but you. Now they got counselors over to that there school that can tell you how to get a Ph.D., if ya wants one."

"Thanks," said the young fellow. Before he left, he asked, "Hey, Mr. Ted, what did you do when you were in Nevada?"

The old man took a swig of sherry and frowned.

"Let's see now. . . . I worked my daddy's spread some . . . an' I prospected for gold and silver, worked in the rodeo . . . was in the calvary for a spell . . . and was a deputy marshal . . ."

"A marshal!"

"Yeah . . . where ya think mah pension comes from? Ya youngsters think all we niggers did was pick cotton in the ole days, huh? There's a lot you should find out about colored people, son . . . and a lot you better find out about yourself."

The school was found easily by the directions Mr. Ted gave him. After a wait of half an hour he saw a counselor who discussed with him his plans for the future. He found that he only had to remain in that school for one semester before he could receive a California high school diploma, if he passed a G.E.D. test, due to his service background, his business and college prep schools, and could then enter college.

"The registration fee here is fifty cents and the board of education textbooks are free of charge," said the counselor. It was some of the best news that he had gotten for some time.

It was dark when he returned to the big house. A light was on the porch and when he started to enter the gate to the back of the house a woman's voice called him.

"Son . . . oh, you there, son!"

It was Mrs. Parsons. It was the first time she had spoken to him like that. He stopped and looked up at her.

"Yes, ma'm," he said.

"Son, the reverend told me to tell you that his cousin is coming tonight from down home. The reverend said he just got the wire today and is expectin' him anytime now. So we'll have to have your room."

"I see," the young man said. "Well, as soon as I get my things I'll be gone."

"Your bags are here, son. The reverend didn't want to bother you none, so they're here on the porch."

He walked up on the porch and found his bags. Lifting them, he said, "Good night, Mrs. Parsons."

"Good-bye, son. My prayers go with you. Bless you."

He thanked her for the hospitality of the house and disappeared into the night.

Now allow me to restate my refrain. And don't misperceive me. My relations with women aren't only that of an exploiter of their flesh and a crusher of their spirits. I'm actually a lover. And I love to love and be all things that a man can be in a love involvement with a woman. But in the same breath I'll tell anyone that I want what I want and that's the name of the game. And when the game deals with female meat, I'm out to score, baby. Make no mistake about it. I wouldn't lie to you. I love being in love and having a lovely lady to release myself in and fondle and fantasize about and free her from ever feeling that she is not the most important thing in the world to me, at least while I am getting into her and getting around her and just being her man. For I am very reluctant to rape any woman I don't relate to.

Figueroa widens past U.S.C., and on the night of the party Jay's little Dodge spurted along the right-hand lane toward the party place. The sky had a deepening indigo covering spread from border to horizon, and inky blue was creeping from the eastern rim. *Swish, swish* . . . the parked cars on our right made that sound as we sped past, the palm branches above their tops reaching sometimes toward the street with the cropped emerald lawns smoothing outward from the trees' cork-tinted bases back between the concrete walks of the red, industrial-style university buildings.

"We have blocks to go," I said.

"Oh, damn, Steve, this part of town always confuses me. I forget we have to go past the park and stadium."

And on we drove down broad Figueroa, the Saturday-evening jam pressing in, the cars searching out ball games, bowling alleys or movies, or going to homes in south L.A., and even farther, to places with names like Inglewood.

We were looking for Len's party, and it was our first time down that part of town since the summer. The last time had been the night of the beach party, after the sweltering day with its short heavy blasts of ocean breezes prodding time along like a coal scow and the bonfire-lit evening with the guys singing and debating above the breakers' rushing drone to get the girls' eyes, and on our way back into town—past the missile manufacturers and safely through lily-white Inglewood—without a traffic ticket, ten of us, six guys and four girls, had stopped at Len's place on Figueroa for a nightcap, bleary-eyed, sand- and sun-worn.

Len had suggested going by his place and helping him with a new gallon of wine, and once inside, with his newest African records setting the beat and the Oscar Brown, Jr., and Nina Simone sides that few of us had heard before, we grabbed at the damp girls and twisted in the shadowy room, ignoring the grit in the folds and crevices of our bodies and swimsuits, and all resolutions of taking it easy now that Labor Day had had it for that year.

Though it really was the same party as that afternoon, Len assured everyone, the same that had begun that morning when someone had found that a lot of people didn't have anything to do the last holiday before school began, so why stop partying now since the slim hugging girls were swilling most of Len's red wine and eating the leftover hot dogs and his sandwiches, getting that fat look about their mouths.

"You better tell these broads to lay off the dogs and sandwiches if these poor slobs are going to make a meal tomorrow," Willy had said. Jay's brother, Willy, was an intense boy, as dark as Jay but with a mean streak hidden most of the time by his quietness.

I hadn't met most of the people before that day; I knew some of the guys—Jay and Willy from being neighbors and I was looking forward to going to college with them—but knew no others well because I hadn't been in town long, but I liked Len and his girl, Lou, especially—they were my friends and guests—and I had suggested giving the leftover food to them; I knew that Len wasn't working and had money problems.

So Jay and I rode searching out Len's place that evening, days after Thanksgiving, and time lay before us to forget books and exams and letters unanswered through the year. Forget the sweep of the second hands on all the timepieces except our own internal gauges, and forget the spin of our senses tuned to the spiral of the seasons which measured the length of lives of men in vacation times and newspaper-headlined obituaries, all never really forgotten, streaming past our private visions like clouds across the new moon.

Forget . . . forgetting for me was all of my past; the past that I daily denied by convincing myself that I was bigger than my past, or the memory of it. What was I doing in my mid-twenties in the first year of college? Could I begin a new life within the shadow of the past ten?

84

What was this new life to be? Did I have a future, and what was it to be? Could anybody like myself expect a future?

My younger friends and classmates, they *knew* what they were going to be and all they would do. Some of them were even grooming themselves to become leaders. I was old enough to be merely a skeptic. Would I someday find myself a leader? And who would be my followers and where would we go?

I guess even then I had a dual inkling, a realization which was fragmented and in opposition to its parts. On one hand was the chance for me to gain knowledge and a profession, and on the other was the private record of experience in how futile and worthless that goal was for me. Would the worth of my new status give my insides a boost in value? But all these were no admitted notions then. I just didn't think about it. In fact, I hardly thought about anything except my glowing future. It was part of the not understood ritual that I hardly allowed to come to the surface, that the suspected myths are but flimsy figments of defense, and that by accepting the dream I knew was fantasy, then the dream must evolve from myth into the reality of hypocrisy. I lived a life I never believed in during that unforgettable past, and those brief years in which Rick, Len and college were part of my experience were like a deranged dream projected from the mind of an idiot. I should have known better than to believe.

I should have known. Wasn't I matured? Some men still pretended me a boy, but I was a man. I knew more than most of my contemporaries, I told myself then. I knew better than to be taken in by my own dream. I was only there to play along with the game. I knew what was what—who owned the oil, the minerals, the air time, the utilities, the lobbies, the stuff. I knew up from down, and where *in* was and who were always out. Didn't I know these things before the game began? I was too hip, I told myself then, to be conned by the same myths spread in the same and in more modern ways. I knew something after so long traveling and from so far. Or did I only glimpse something else lying beneath the surface words of the volumes I had read, some smudges between the clear lines, and was I and am I now completely a fool?

Thinking it over again, I believe that I've always known too much.

When he arrived back with his old friends, they had changed. Six years made a difference. Jack was balding, his cowlicks met at the center of his scalp, and he looked ten years older than his late twenties. Marie was a mother and fat. The little boys were off to college, now picketing and sitting in at Woolworth's in a large city miles away. Uncle Clyde was semiretired, which meant he drew a social security check because of his high blood pressure but was able to go alone to the supermarket and cash it for the monthly groceries. But Aunt Bessie looked the same. What gray she had earned through the years was now hidden by a wig.

The farm didn't exist as it did before. It was kept as a summer resort place for city colored folks, and was used as a quiet retreat by the family during the off-season. They lived in town now, close to Jack's and Marie Ann's jobs. Marie worked in the noiseless plant just outside of town in its own little industrial park; she made parts for something she called "classified information." She was between husbands then, with two kids, and since she worked for her own living, and those of her children, bringing home, mind you, more than most men she knew, she wasn't ready to get involved with just any man so easily, not even a summer sweet daddy like Dandy. She was quite independent.

Jack worked at the refinery and was buying a home in town like Aunt Bess and Marie Ann were. He and his wife, Ida, were broken up. She had gone north, leaving the children with him; he seemed to like it that way.

Jack and his old friend would sit upon his porch in the early evening, after Jack had gotten off from work and wolfed down a huge meal with his guest and then broken open a couple of cans of beer. Jack would tell him how there wasn't nothing that he needed; he had everything in the world he wanted, a home, kids, a good job, and he even bragged about pickings in the local-women department.

"You should see all the women bustin' their rumps to take care of me and my brats, Dandy. Man, I don't have to worry about who's gonna fix my dinner or get my clothes to the laundry or sew a button on my shirt. Yeah, I give Aunt Bess more than enough out of my pay check to take care of us all, her and Uncle Clyde included, but you know Bessie; she wouldn't do nothin' for nobody that she couldn't get somebody else to do. And she can really get these little church and factory gals to take care of her 'big son' and her little 'grand-children.' They all horny as hell and lookin' for somethin' to do anyway."

They talked as dusk fell, until the biggest event of the evening took place, the rounding of the corner of the Greyhound bus, headed north, pulling away from its stop around the corner next to the post office. The bus would pass without either of them saying a word, then Jack and his friend would go inside and watch TV and drink more beer until some girl came to the porch door for Jack and after some whispered conversation between them for a minute, he would come back and say:

"I'm gonna take a little walk, ole buddy. Don't worry about lockin' up or turnin' out anything if you decide to go to bed before I get back. This is a country town, ya know. The kids are over Aunt Bessie's for the evenin'. Sleep tight. See you tomorrow."

Jack's friend might sit there in front of the TV for a while and watch the lighted rectangle as if he were looking at it, then wander into the kitchen for one last one for the road, and finally go up to his room.

He could have stayed out on the farm; there wasn't much traffic out there that time of year, he was told. But he preferred being near people, the ones he knew a little at least.

His days were spent over to Aunt Bess and Uncle Clyde's. He could still hold interesting conversations with Bess, even more inter-esting than he remembered having with her before, when she thought of him as a boy. Now, at least to his way of thinking, she had one of the brightest, most entertaining minds of those people in the town that he had met. Uncle Clyde mistook him for someone else the day he arrived and still confused him with that person, so hesitated at speaking too much to him, for fear of embarrassment. But Dandy did go with him to shop one time. And was helpful in carrying the cases and cartons and sacks of provisions that were adequate enough in quantity to feed them all, some other guests included, for much longer than a month.

"Always be prepared is my motto, Dickie," explained Uncle Clyde to him.

One night while looking at TV with Jack, and while holding his older honorary niece, who looked strikingly like his oldest daughter, on his knee, two young women came to the porch door. He learned a couple of weeks later that one of the girls had been planning to come for him, since seeing him his first day in town, but that was after he was spending most of his nights over to her house, a small two-storied place with a single bedroom at the top of the stairs with a feather down mattress where he lay with the cute plump factory girl in sexual bliss. She had a small child who slept in the middle of a large couch downstairs, but being used to children and lonely without their presence near, he didn't mind his new woman rising in the middle of the night and nursing her baby.

His mail caught up with him and he got his retirement pay from the post office and treated his friends and sweetheart to whatever they wanted. Jack wanted a bottle of bourbon, 100 proof, and Jack's two little girls got colored dolls. Aunt Bess, Uncle Clyde and Marie Ann ignored him. His girl friend couldn't make up her mind, so he bought her a nightgown downtown so sheer that she giggled at her gift and hid it in her bottom drawer before snapping off the night light and undressing and slipping nudely under the covers of their soft bed to thank him for his generosity.

He got bored by the time fall drew near. After waiting several days until he was sure that his sexy girl's monthly period had appeared, he said good-bye to Aunt Bess, handed her some money, which she could always use, and was on the bus when it rounded the corner that evening, passing Jack's house. Jack was in his usual place, wearing a thin jacket, rocking in his favorite chair, a beer in his hand, probably waiting to shoot the breeze with his old buddy. Jack didn't see him when the darkened bus passed.

The bus rolled slowly over the railroad tracks, then picked up speed, and he was out of the city limits in four minutes.

"Hi there, Steve," the thin girl said, opening the door. A rush of sound backed her narrow face, which was drawn angular as a horse's and was wedged like an ax with a Spanish hint that all combined into an attractive girl.

"Lou, how are you?" I said to Len's girl.

The party noises of jazz and shoes and laughter and speech swept out into the courtyard of the apartment where we stood; Lou's magic of smile and brashness and the party clamor grabbed at Jay and me, pulling us inside. "Things are just gettin' good, baby," she said. "Ya just lookin' sawh nice, Steve."

Her New York Puerto Rican accent was a fine point; it gave fact to her exotic features.

"Thanks, Lou. You remember Jay, don't you?"

She greeted Jay, nodding, smiling, as she led us into the living room. "Oh, yeah, you were at the beach party Labor Day," she said. "I saw ya dere."

Red and blue lights lit the first room, where groups stood talking, some holding cans of beer or glasses; almost all had cigarettes glowing in the dim room like tiny signal lights. A radio in a mahogany console played soft jazz, and from the back room could be heard a hi-fi and dancing.

"Friends." Len separated himself from a group and shook hands, holding both of his in a cup over our rights as we shook. I had never seen a fraternal shake like that before.

A knock sounded at the front door and Lou left to answer, her purple leotards flashing below the green corduroy skirt.

"How have you people been?" Len asked, grinning, his straggling beard having grown more and his great head of hair seeming two inches longer, falling down his neck. And before we answered:

"Here, have one," he said, having gone to a table holding a large tin tub and pulling out two cans of Amber & Brauer beer and bringing them opened to us.

"The white man must be exterminated, they must go, for their time is drawing near," a voice said in the crowd after Len had moved away toward the new arrivals.

"Let's see what this is all about, Benson," Jay suggested.

The group was standing in an alcove which separated the two rooms and the bathroom entrance huddled in one corner. The red and blue lights from the front, an orange from the bathroom and dim crimson falling from the back shone about the group. A tall brown youth stood in the center with about half a dozen quieter people about him.

"The time is near and all must stand up and be counted. . . . Those against us will have to go with the devils," the youth said.

"Yeah, man, that's right, man," a shorter, darker, slim youth said, standing to his side.

Jay and I slid among the group, between two girls.

"But how do you propose to get your black nation here in America?" one of the girls asked.

"How do we expect to get a black nation!" the tall one exclaimed as if he couldn't believe his ears. "We'll get it because our ancestors have spilled their blood in this white man's land for hundreds and hundreds of years. . . ."

"That isn't what I asked you," the girl said. She had a bright gingerbread look about her and was tall without her heels.

"But that *is* what you asked me, sister," the tall one said. "Now let's go on. . . . How did America come to be?"

"That's not the point," someone said.

"Why don't you answer me?" the girl asked.

"Listen, baby," the smaller youth cut in, talking to the girl, "what you don't understand is . . ."

"Why don't you let the girl speak?" Jay said.

The slim one turned to Jay; his head glistened in the lights, for his

90

hair was almost completely cut off. "Listen, man, when I want to hear from you, I'll ask."

He had been drinking and when he spoke his swaying gave his voice an approaching, receding tone.

"Why don't you let someone else speak?" I said.

"Listen, man, shut up!" he said, now glaring and leaning toward me.

"This is all irrelevant," the tall one said in a prissy way, attempting to tidy up the scene.

"I'd just like to know why don't you let someone say something?" I said. Both Jay and I had drunk our first beer fast and changed to wine, and Jay was grinning at me, getting a lot of pleasure from the exchange, but he didn't realize that these guys were on the edge of fighting. I wondered if in Jay's narrow life he had ever been forced to fight. I just knew he wasn't a fighter and these boys were and would if I didn't get things settled. I didn't come to fight; neither would I back down yet.

"I'm telling you for the last time, man, shut up!" the boy said, louder.

"But how can I get a word in edgewise if I do that?" I smiled as I said it; no use going into a fight with the other guys knowing you're nervous.

"Shut up, man!"

"Well, what do we have here?" Len stepped in. "A little civic affairs debate?" He took my arm and led me away. "Here, I have someone for you to meet."

I tried to catch at least one of the girls' eyes before I left but they were both again talking with the tall boy; Jay was cornered by the shorter and was nodding, fingering his glasses, like the campus intellectual he was. Maybe there wouldn't have been a hassle.

"Who are those guys?" I asked.

"Oh, they're some Black Nationalist friends."

I was interested. The only Black Nationalists I had ever heard of in years were in the newspapers. Could these be Black Muslims? No, I thought. I read that Muslims don't drink, so I guessed that they weren't, but they really sounded different from anything I had heard in a decade.

"Yeah. . .you'll know. . . yes, indeed *. . . when it hits ya . . .* yes, indeed *. . . you'll scream 'n' holler, yes, indeed . . .* yes, indeed *. . ."* the phonograph played for the twisting dancers.

"Here . . . you look like you need this," Len had said to the girl standing against the wall watching the dancers; he offered her a beer and presented me with the same motion; she accepted us both.

"His name is Steve," he said as Lou walked into the room and pulled him aside to whisper.

"Hi," I said, "and yours?"

"Lenarrd . . . you give the best parties in town . . . Evaaryboody's here!" a female shrieked from somewhere in the house, and the sound of smashing glass came from the kitchen.

I saw Lou slap Len in the face; the sound smacked above the party din, and I turned away as the girl told me her name was Mona.

"Yeah, you'll holler, yes, indeed . . . yes, indeed *. . ."*

Cowbells clattered; Lou went out the door and Len turned toward me shaking his head and scowling. I lowered mine. The dancers seemed not to notice anything but themselves. More people crowded into the nine-by-twelve room, followed by Lou, who rejoined Len. I asked Mona to dance but she said she'd rather watch and talk and drink.

"What do you do?" she asked, as someone's elbow hunched her in the back and shoved her into me. She squeezed closer and I put my arm about her as a shield.

"Have ya ev'va hurd ah uh tag team drinkin' match?" someone in another corner drunkenly asked his group.

"Nawh," his drinking partner answered.

"Well, ya see, ya get sum guys ahround'a table, see?" he continued. "Ya got tree glasses on da table, see?"

"Yeah, okay, I see."

I stood with my back to the wall beside Mona. She came a little above my head, but she had on heels. She was slim and had a clean smile in a golden face with slight Oriental-cast eyes that sparkled.

"I'm going to school now," I told her.

"So am I."

We found that we went to the same college.

"Ya gonna feel it down ta ya soul . . . yes, indeed . . . *Ya gonna know it's dat good ole rock 'n' roll* . . . yes, indeed."

Lou's eyes sparkled. They were in open argument, with her shaking her head and Len's light tan face darkening under the ruby lights.

"They're brown glasses, see?" the guy continued in the corner.

"Yeah, brown glasses," his buddy repeated, "like da kind ya get in da fiv'ven ten."

"Yeah, dat's right! 'n' ya got wah-ta in one, Tundderburd wine in one, an' gin in da ud'da."

"I haven't been to a party like this in a long time," said Mona.

"Do you like it?"

"It's great!" She drank another swallow and clutched my arm when one of the girl dancers made an extremely suggestive movement, bumping her tight-clad rear to make the fabric seem about to burst.

"Can you do that?" I asked.

"Well . . . I guess so, but not in public." She clapped her hand to her mouth after the words were out, and we had our best laugh that night.

93

"Yes, indeed . . . yes, indeed *. . . yes, indeed . . ."*

"Yeah, yeah . . . an' whatcha do af'ta dat?"

"Well, ya start off countin', see? Round da table clockwise . . . 'n' da one dat calls a number which is ah multiple ah sev'van has ta drink one ah da glasses."

"Ah multee . . . wha?"

"Ah multiple! Ya know . . . like turtee-five or sev'van-tee-sev'van . . . en'nyting dat sev'van goes inta."

"Yeah . . . I see, like moosical chairs."

Len was dancing with a small girl. Her hair was cut short and she wore sandals and shoved her breasts out like they were weapons. Lou wasn't in the room.

In the front of the house, someone turned the radio on as loud as possible, and from its twin speakers: *"George? I joined the Money-plan today!"* a feminine voice said.

"Yeah . . . ya begin wit' one, den two an' tree . . ."

"Whatcha do when ya cum ta sev'van?"

"Hmmm . . . dear? That's nice," a radio husband voice said.

"Ya say 'pass' when sev'van cums up, see? 'n' da ud'da guy sez 'ate' 'n' da nex' sez 'nine.' "

"With Moneyplan I get more earning power," radio lady said.

Len still danced, picking up his tempo when voices began screaming for him to turn the radio off. Mona placed her head against my chest to shut out the din, but the noise didn't bother everyone.

"Yeah, I saw sum guys get up'ta da nineties af'fore sum-bahty loses an' has ta drink one ah da glasses."

94

"How 'bout if he chooses da wah-ta?"

"He don' know, see? They're mixed up."

"That sounds great, dear. With so much more earning power, no one can afford to be without Moneyplan," radio gentleman answered.

Jay came into the room holding his ears and grimacing and smiling as at an entire circus. The tall girl followed, and they began twisting on the far side of the room.

"That's really great. Wait ta nex' Sad'dee night when I have my gig."

"Yeah . . . but be sure ta mix da glasses up good. . . . If ya got a lush in da crowd, he'll slip da most times an' get da gin."

"Yeah . . . dat's right. . . . I'll mix 'em up good."

"That's right, darling, everyone should have Moneyplan!"

"I can see some sonna a bitch gettin' da Tundderburd. . . . I hopes da red-eyed pig joins Alkies Anonomuss af'ta dat. . . ."

"Yeah, man, wait ta nex' week."

"Won't it ever stop?" Mona lifted her head and pleaded.

"I can't see . . ."

"What did you say?"

"I can't see how they can keep it up!" I told her.

"Dear? What are we going to do with all our Moneyplan money?" radio husband asked.

"Shove it up your ass!" someone screamed and the radio was turned off to wails of laughter.

"Den I'll put all wah-tas in dem 'n' choke da crud."

"Now ya tinkin', buddy boy, now ya yous'sin ya skull."

"I'm glad that's over," Mona said, wiping the tears from her eyes. "Well, I'll have to be going."

"Already?"

"Yes." She smiled.

"When will I see you again?" I asked.

We made a date for the first day after school reconvened, after she told me I couldn't come by her house.

"Let me walk you home."

"No, there's a telephone booth at the corner and I can have my husband drive over and pick me up, if he's there," she said. "It's only a few blocks." She touched my hand and was gone.

The record was changed; Len still danced with the same girl; they put on a show, with the other dancers opening a small space for their churning bodies. Lou was back in the room with her eyes at the back of Len's neck, and she caught me looking her way and she flashed her sweet little horsy grin. I wanted to go over and dance with her but I didn't.

I had just decided to move across the room and ask Jay if he was ready to leave when the door jarred outside, and a loud hallooing came through it with noise of movement. Lou spun and ran from the room, and I heard her voice and laughter mingled with the babble. I walked through the door into the red and blue room and saw Rick, who I didn't know then, dancing violently with Lou, his head shining and the colored lights shimmering upon his plastic glasses frame and upon the lenses and his teeth.

I thought I'd stay awhile longer.

After his wife left with his children, and before he broke ties with his mother, he spent some time with some of his cousins, the few children he had grown close to as a child and kept the connection of family and friendship strong with throughout the years. They were all sons and daughters of his aunt Bernell, who had helped raise him.

His oldest male cousin was in the army, in Europe, and Elvin, who had been like a younger brother to him, was at that stage when women and the adventures of their pursuit and capture were the paramount activities in his life, so he didn't intrude upon Elvin's love life, but spent time with one of Elvin's sisters, Dinah, and formed a solid drinking relationship with her husband, Harry.

They would all go to neighborhood bars, dances and cabarets, and he would flirt with the foxes encountered and sometimes take along one of the girls that worked in the laundry with Dinah, and he and Harry would have long rambling arguments about boxing before the bars closed and Harry had to get home and catch a nod so that he could get up and reach his job at dawn in a bakery. Dinah and Harry didn't have any children, being that Dinah could never have any, and would one day leave Harry through frustration and finally find a man with five motherless kids, but she and Harry did not know this then, so were having their good times while they could before they got tied down, but they both liked their cousin Steve very much, and liked to drink with him and keep his mind off of his troubles.

One night, just before closing, Dinah, Harry and he left a café not far from where they lived, being that Steve lived within blocks of them, and they were in good spirits.

He and Harry had been drinking screwdrivers, introducing Dinah to the drink, and they had sipped and gotten high, observing Sugar

97

Ray Robinson on TV knock somebody through the ropes so hard with a left hook that he didn't return.

While strolling home on that summer night, the traffic lights seldom needed on the empty avenue, they harmonized, Little Esther and Johnnie Otis style, and Harry spotted a cat and threw rocks at it, running ahead of his wife and her cousin.

Dinah's cousin remained beside her and laughed with her at her husband's comic movements in his mock rage at the small animal.

"Don't hurt him, honey. . . . Please don't hurt the poor little thing," said Dinah.

But Harry had stalked the alley beast into a vacant lot.

Coming toward Dinah and her cousin was a dark thin youth of their age, and when he got abreast of Dinah he reached out his hand and took her arm and said, "Don't I know you, baby?"

Pulling away, Dinah said, "Nawh, man, I don't know you." And she moved behind her cousin.

The stranger reached after her and being still in good condition, Dinah's cousin knocked him down and semiconscious with a hard right dig in the solar plexus and a sharp uppercut with the same hand right on the wise-ass's jaw.

Turning, the cousin and Dinah continued up the street nonchalantly, leaving the rude one lying in the shadows of the billboard that hung over the corner lot, out of which Harry had emerged a second before, seeing only the blows delivered and the victim fall.

"What happened, man?" asked Harry.

"I had to knock that punk out."

"That guy touched me, baby," Dinah said.

"He did, huh?" Harry said and turned and ran back to stomp the wife-molester.

"Wait, honey . . ." Dinah said and followed.

The body moved in the shadows and when Harry entered the dark to kick it, Dinah and her cousin heard "Owww . . ." And then they saw Harry fall backwards toward them, onto the lighted part of the sidewalk.

"Watch it, Steve," Harry said, curled up clutching his middle. "He's got a knife."

Dinah screamed. And her cousin descended upon the criminal like a mad bull. He closed with the assailant in a two-hand-and-foot attack. He threw everything he had at his attacker: hooks, right crosses, jabs, bolos, butts in the clinches, feet in the stomach, knee-caps and groin, but he was jabbin' 'n' movin' like pretty Sugar Ray while his human punching bag was stabbin'. He hurt the other man badly before the knife caught up with him. That night he wasn't carrying any weapons, not even a fingernail file, but he had been faking and reaching for his pocket between kicks and blows, as if he had a weapon there, to keep his adversary off, who was pressing in for the kill, but he was really trying to get his belt off as he pretended to be drawing his equalizer, for then he would have a deadly weapon in hand too, when it felt like he had been struck in the throat by a stick. He coughed, recovering, he thought, and charged the knifer, knocking him down again. Almost immediately the man was up and racing down the street with him in chase, but strangely he was short of breath and couldn't follow as fast, then he slowed and felt the river of warmth running down his shirt front. He looked down and saw his chest covered with the blood that was spilling from the gash in his throat. Then he heard behind him Dinah scream, "Stop, Steve! Stop! Harry's hurt! He's dying. Stop!"

He turned and stumbled back to the couple; Dinah screamed when she saw his condition and he had to waste precious energy by shouting at her to keep her head and not faint.

"If you go out on us, Dinah, me and Harry are dead! Dead, you understand? We got to get to the hospital!"

They dragged and carried each other the three blocks to Dinah's mother's house. Not a police car passed, though a cab slowed when they hailed but sped away when the driver saw their tragedy.

Dinah's mother came out of the house after hearing her name screamed by her daughter as the trio entered the block. She leaned over the banister of her front porch and asked what could she do?

"Mom, they have to get to the hospital! Quick, Mom! Get your car keys and drive us to the hospital!" Dinah screamed at her mother.

Her mother disappeared inside and Harry groaned, fell and passed out. Steve held his neck with a handkerchief swollen by his blood, and tried to remain calm and slow down his movements. Dinah was crying uncontrollably, trying to revive Harry, bending over him like she was giving him the last rites and artificial respiration at the same time.

"Which hospital should I go?" Dinah's mother asked when she came out of the house extremely confused. But she carried packs of old newspapers which she soon spread over her car seats before anyone was allowed to get in.

"The closest one, Aunt Bernell," Steve croaked calmly.

Pulling Harry, they dragged and lifted him into the front seat, Dinah jumped in beside him, then Steve crawled into the back and lay upon his back across the newspapers, feeling his life seep out before he lost consciousness.

And the last thing before he died, he heard his aunt say, "Don't get any blood on my seat covers. Watch the seat covers. Please don't get any blood on them," as she pulled the late model Oldsmobile out from the curb and sped away on her mission of mercy.

There were only the talkers left in the front room. Rick and Lou had moved to the back room to dance. They parted after one dance and found separate partners. Rick danced with almost every girl; it seemed that he had to have each girl on the floor with him that night. Len danced seriously with a few, never with Lou, improvising steps,

100

and all the while smiling at his partners. Few others danced. The spectators crowded the walls watching the couples under the scarlet glare of the lights, and Afro-Cuban records played long drum solos with the pairs dancing wildly as the tempo rose. In his black suit and white bow tie, the glare of the room a pink sheen on his shirt, Rick's costume contrasted to Len's Levi's, sandals and ballooning black fuzzy sweater.

Outside, the talkers settled the problems of the world. A dark young man with a face like a skin-covered skull stood holding Jay's and the tall girl's attention. He wore glasses on his bony face and smiled whenever he believed he made his point.

"Why, yesss, sister," he said to the girl, "the name 'Negro' is an invention of the white man to relegate brother to an inferior position. . . ."

"But how does the name 'Afro-American' or just 'blackman' make you more American?" the girl asked.

"It's not that it makes us anything, especially American, sister; it is what we really are and should be called," the dark man said. He had a way of slightly extending his hands forward when he was about to smile and then when the point was made he flicked his hands over, showing his palms upwards. It was a gesture to say, "Here, take this, you need it!"

"We don't want to become better Americans," he continued, "for we have no country and know we aren't Americans at all . . . or do you believe that you're an American, sister?"

She looked at him.

When she was about to reply, he said, ". . . and if you are, then what class . . . ha ha ha . . ."

"You're completely off the subject, *maan,*" Jay said.

Words like "man" or "cat" or "hip" were special to Jay. He pronounced them with an accent. It was as if he had not learned the words until he was grown and was experiencing life through foreign eyes, and upon a far continent, so each time he said his special words, it seemed he should first have said: "How do *you* people say

101

'man'?" Talking to Jay, at times, was almost like viewing a character from an old movie, the foggy London or Orient Express kind that comes on late at night on television.

It was then that I knew I had discovered something that I didn't understand completely before. Not only Jay but most everyone I knew played parts, had roles. This wasn't too startling, for the same had been explained to me many times before in classes and by books but now I had discovered it for myself, and it all seemed weird, then, with the drum music and beer and wine, and all the players standing there, drinking and dancing in their masks, their disguises contrived in split seconds for the moment. But where Jay played his role subtly most of the time, coming on with his black genteel cultured slightly continental role, others played their parts openly, like the skull-faced guy Jay and the girl talked to. Looking around then, I suspected that most that night played as their parts demanded, and few knew or perhaps none except myself.

There were other talkers in the room; the slim dark boy of earlier talked to a plump girl. They sat upon the couch and he wagged his finger seriously as he spoke. Convinced, the girl nodded.

"What school did he go to?" a large-headed boy asked his group.

"Southern," one of them said.

"Yeah?" another joined in. "Then he must be pretty heavy."

"Awwhhh, he don't look so heavy to me," the first boy said. "If he thinks he's so heavy just let him come over here and I'll cut him up."

"Who are you to cut up anyone, man?"

"Yeah, listen to ole waterhead Willy here," another one said. "Go get that boy."

In the kitchen Lou pushed me aside.

"Steve, I want you to stay tonight." Her big eyes rolled beneath her mascaraed lids and the whites were very clear.

"Do you think I should ask Len?"

"Don't ask that mahthafukker anything," she said. "It'll be okay." She talked low and secret. "Please, Steve."

I wondered where I would sleep as I walked back into the living room. There was a narrow leather couch. The floor was covered by a pale grass rug, with cloth and leather pillows against the wall.

Rick was back in the room and most groups had combined to surround him but he stepped out of the center and to one side, addressing people, sometimes bending to those sitting upon the floor or on pillows, answering queries, shaking hands and walking among the crowd like a politician running for office.

I remembered where I had seen him before. One place had been at school earlier in the year. Not just one time but many times. He ran for student office in our college.

"Hello," the small brown boy had said. "My name's Ricardo Evans. I'm running for president of the student council. I would like you to vote for me."

He made his practiced speech in a funny little voice and gave me a pin and cardboard tag with his name, "Ricardo S. Evans for President." I took it, thanking him, and dropped it in the first trash can I passed. It wasn't hard forgetting Ricardo S. Evans until three weeks later.

Marco Polo Henderson and I lived on a palm-lined street beside the Hollywood Freeway. Our two-bedroom apartment was upstairs over the mostly absent landlord's flat. The landlord found it necessary to be missing from his buxom wife and two kids the majority of the time because he worked full time as a sports car mechanic and kept a girl in a Western Avenue apartment who was possessive, as well as being young, slim and without children. His extended stays taught his wife how to collect our rent, clean and decorate our bachelor quarters, and determine what other needs of her tenants she could attend to, all without aid from her husband.

Marco Polo and I attended the same school. At the time our ambitions didn't seem too dissimilar. We made almost perfect roommates: we didn't like the same type girls, our friends loathed one another and would hardly have anything to do with us separately when one or the other was about, and we did almost nothing together except gamble and meet each afternoon after classes at the chess tables.

It was in the school patio at the table where our chess group met. A canopy covered the tables and benches, shielding us from the sun. The regulars and drift-ins were there every day, and we played for low stakes. I played with the class "D" players for fifty cents, being I'm about a "C—" player, and Marc played for better stakes of a buck or two, for he was one of the near best.

I was the only one who beat him regularly. Afternoons, to get things going, I would generally play a game with Marc, and if a new face showed among the kibitzers and asked for winners, Marc lost a close game to me. Nine out of ten of the new players beat me easily the first game, though being determined, I played my opponents a better game the next time, and then one last with the same results except that I had just about pulled it out of the fire in the end game.

Having destroyed me and pocketed my two bucks, the winner would nearly always ask Marc, if he hadn't been tagged yet, "Hey, buddy, how about a game?"

That's the way the blond all-American types would say it, usually upping the stakes. Marc's a natural mime and he would shoot back in the fellow's own voice, "Well, buddy, I don't see why not."

That's how we made our bus fare and cigarette money.

One afternoon one of the new players threatened to turn our gambling in to the dean of gambling or whatever dean takes care of that sort of thing. After Marc returned his ten bucks and the sucker had left, someone had gotten the idea of forming our loose group into a campus club. It was to be for our greater benefit, or so they said, by being sanctioned under the school charter. Among other compliances, we found that we had to collect dues before we were allowed on campus. We had been meeting together for months for profit and comradeship; then we tell a dean that we want to get into the yearbook and maybe represent the school in intercollegiate matches, and we find that we're illegal. So we had to collect dues, find a name, which finally was the Chess Club, get an adviser and elect officers.

I was the first president of the Chess Club to attend our college's Associated Men's Smoker.

After the dinner of burnt beef, and before the entertainment, which was to be several cheerleaders wearing hula skirts over shorts, doing the twist in turtleneck sweaters with school letters pasted on, and two myopic linemen from the football team in a wet pillow fight with we elected officials on the sidelines with cream pies to assist our favorites, some dean of something made a speech about fellowship, excellence and manliness, and announced: "Gentlemen: I give you your new student body president, Mr. Ricardo S. Evans."

Applause and cheers deafened me, with me even joining in, as it seemed the right thing to do, and after the crowd quieted, Rick stepped to the podium wearing a dark suit and white bow tie. He nodded to some he knew in the audience and took a white sheet of paper from his inside suit pocket. His plastic-rimmed glasses shone under the spot and he stuck out his chest, a gesture that I would come to know well.

"Good evening, gentlemen," he started, and glancing over to the waiting cheerleaders, he added, "and ladies . . . ha ha ha. My topic tonight is . . ."

He had begun and just as he began there were titters in the audience. He paused and smiled a moment and then continued, and there was more and louder laughing. I wondered if there was a supreme joke or some game being played. What were they laughing at? I thought, and by *they* I meant the white boys. What was so hilarious? Rick and I were the only negroes there, so why were they laughing when he stood before them? I became furious. Rick began again and the snickers started; the dean stirred and a partial hush fell, and Rick continued once more; the giggles were with him throughout his speech. I didn't even hear what he had to say.

They are laughing at *him,* I thought; those little white bastards are laughing at a colored boy who stands before them as a man. Someone who represented them. I wanted to shout and grab the nearest white throat. I could even have throttled the dean. And I wanted Rick to get down. I wanted him to just leave their white faces laughing and let them get on with their costumed untouchable pompon girls and have their muscle and cream pie orgy without their pure and boyish innocence being damaged. I wanted to scream. I wanted him to help me kill them. I wanted him to come out into the audience and begin swinging, not wet pillows, but knives, fists and feet. Kill them first, I thought, but don't let them chuckle at your manhood and giggle at your natural nobility; don't let them think you a joke for competing with them and being something and doing what few others could. I thought: *Kill them! Kill them! Let's kill them, Rick, brother! Two blackmen are more than a match for a hundred soft-minded, weak-faced college whites.* But I only thought and remained silent, and we didn't act out my dream, not that night.

As the only other black in the large room, one who would have raved and ranted and threatened and cursed and drawn blood in the hallowed halls of the academy, I suddenly felt contempt for Rick when he smiled and went on with his speech. And I felt contempt for myself for sitting there among them while they laughed, felt contempt from not standing amongst them and with my steak knife stabbing each and all in his white smugness that night of the cheerless cheerleaders and orgiastic athletes. I felt hate, the hate that had propelled me to see only ahead to a new future, not believing in the past or present filled with ignorance, violence, cruelty and ridicule. I was so filled those moments that I never heard Rick, nor suspected until months later that they were laughing at him because he was speaking to them in a very proper British accent, one with a refined southern drawl.

"Can I ask you a favor, Steve?" Len asked me when he came in from the back room.

"Sure."

"Will you stay tonight?" He looked concerned. "Lou is a bit dis-traught tonight and when she gets like this I think it's best to have people around she likes. I can never tell what she might do, and when she gets this way anything can happen."

I agreed to stay.

After Len left to speak with Rick, I told Jay that I would not be riding back with him.

"Well, what a pleasant surprise, Benson," he said. "My word, but I'm fortunate tonight. I was planning to take Evelyn home."

He fell into very precise speech when out with girls and his show for the tall girl was complete. One would hardly believe he was from Alabama.

"Yes, the best thing you could do is learn about your homeland," the slim boy told the plump girl. He sagged on the couch, a beer can in his hand.

"Yes, I've been wanting to begin learning about Africa but . . ."

A pudgy boy who had stayed close to Rick now stood alone; the crowd had moved away from him following Rick's jittery path. The boy did a private dance of his own making and pulled a pocket knife from his sleeve with a flourish, opened the shining blade with a snap of the button, and whirled and tossed the blade as he danced. He seemed the youngest in the room. Whenever a girl got near he called out to her and said several phrases before she moved away in the crowd. I hadn't seen him drinking.

"Yes, I'd say that the repressed Oedipal urges in whites cause them to act with hostility toward we blacks. If you'll notice, the most blatant homosexuals are nearly always white," someone told a large-eyed girl.

"Really!" she answered.

"Yes, the keeping of slaves has a definite correlation with masochistic and sadistic tendencies, plus many of the other more severe psychotic traumas. . . ."

"Really!"

The crowd had thinned. Slower records played in the back. My head was light from the drinks.

"Will you dance with me?" Lou asked.

Inside, there were three other couples; Len and the small girl with pointy breasts made one pair. Lou danced as she looked: coarse and brisk with unexpected moments of grace and charm. It was my first time on the floor that night, and with the beers, and not having to compete with the serious dancers, I enjoyed holding Lou in my arms. Len and the other girl stayed to their corner until the record stopped; then he led her over.

"Hello, Steve. I want you to meet Tanya," he said with a slight bow. "Tanya Jefferson, this is Steve Benson."

We changed partners and the next record was another slow one and the small girl felt very close to me.

"Enjoying yourself?" I asked.

"Why, yes. Len is so enjoyable."

She had been in Los Angeles since she was a baby; her family came from Ohio. Her hair was cut short and she smiled a lot. I thought that she must be some sort of Black Nationalist because of her haircut, but she didn't act the part, and I didn't think I should inquire.

Len and Lou argued quietly, with Len shaking his head and widening his mouth to emphasize words as he did when he wished to speak clearly. Lou glared at him, not allowing him to hold her too close. But the evening was becoming right for me.

"Eeee . . . *Oh, gawd*!" came from the front room. We looked around at each other and then Len raced out the door to the front, followed by Lou.

The large-eyed girl stood in the middle of the front room, holding her dress out away from her body. The red sheath had a wide stain down the front.

"He poured beer on me," she said, pointing to the pudgy boy, who stood and grinned against the wall.

Len peered into the girl's face and turned to the boy.

"Brother," he began, and Rick stepped between them.

"There must be some confusion as to the circumstances in what happened here, Lenard," Rick said.

108

"Why the hell he throw that on her for?" Lou shouted.

"But, sister, you weren't here," Rick began.

"When I wouldn't dance with him and told him he acted like a fool he told me I had to drink his beer or wear it, and then he threw it on me when I wouldn't drink," she said while crying.

Rick spoke softly to Len in a corner; some of the crowd muttered. A few went for their coats.

"Take care of yourself, Benson," Jay said, patting me on the back. "Sure you don't need a ride?"

He and the tall girl, Evelyn, left.

"I just want to know why he did it," Lou said. Len tried pushing her across the room; she resisted. "Just get him out of here, the little punk," she yelled from behind Len.

"Sister, why don't you refrain from making inaccurate statements?" Rick asked.

"Go to hell, Rick," she said. "Go to hell!"

The boy started talking to the offended girl in a low voice. He had a round moon face and a glistening coating of scented pomade clung to his hair in pasty patches. I had seen boys like him before, ones who had not been outside their farm communities or small towns until they were in their late teens or older. They were like immigrants from strange lands, carrying secret knowledge that they could not communicate, but were the first ones to pick up the poorer habits of the new culture, faster than they could blend them into their old personalities. Usually the worst aspects of the new showed through in displays of brash behavior, and they sometimes formed rebellious, overbearing natures to cover their inexperience.

Lou talked loudly in the kitchen. "Why do you invite a mahthafukker like that for?"

"Now, Lou Ellen," Len said.

"But, sister . . ." Rick pleaded.

She charged from between them straight to the fat boy. He smiled and waited for her rebuke until her gob of spit splattered against his forehead. I inched forward, hoping the boy wouldn't produce his

109

knife again, but Lou had already spun and stalked into the bathroom, seeing the boy's stare of horror when her spit stuck upon his face. She jerked the bathroom door so violently it shook the house.

The fat boy wiped his face with a large pink handkerchief. Many of the crowd seemed ashamed for him and turned away; more got their coats and said good night.

"My people, my people," the dark man with the skull-like face said.

With the stain drying on her dress, the girl spoke to the pudgy boy. They seemed both to console each other about their separate calamities.

"Lou, open the door," Len said.

"Sister, sister, please." Rick stood with Len and pounded and called out.

"Will she be okay?" the skull-faced one asked.

"I don't know, Jacob," Len answered.

The knocking kept up another five minutes and I got a fresh beer for myself and took Tanya a paper cup of wine in the back room.

"I guess the party's over," she said.

The slim youth and the girl he had been talking with the last part of the evening entered and began kissing. Tanya and I stopped our conversation and went back into the front, but we stayed out of the way of Len, Rick and Jacob, who were deciding if they could take off the bathroom door from their side without splintering the frame. Tanya and I went into the kitchen.

"Do you live far?" I asked.

"No, not too far."

I told her that I had promised to stay overnight but that I could see her home and return. She let me know that Rick was seeing her home.

"Steve," Len said. "Will you please come with me? I want you to help me get Lou out of the bathroom."

I couldn't tell him that I didn't want to get involved.

We went out the kitchen door, which faced the front of the building, and walked past the rows of apartment doors to the end of the

110

court and then turned in back of the units. It was a tight squeeze sliding through the narrow weed-filled space between fence and building.

When we came opposite the rear of his apartment, we peered through a small window.

Lou sat in the bathtub with her arms folded and stared at her ballerina shoes. Her sharp face was poised like a dagger waiting for a sound or a signal, and I wondered what cutting words and tearing of emotions her thin mouth would bring.

"She's all right," Len whispered. "She's cut her wrists and taken overdoses of pills several times."

Back in the apartment, Len called through the door to her. Jacob was sitting on the couch next to the slim boy, and the fat one who had started the trouble and the girl were gone. About ten people remained. The record machine played once more in the back though the beer tub was empty. Someone had opened a gallon jug of red wine.

"Lou, I know it's cold in there," Len said. "Let me give you a blanket. I have a blanket for you, Lou Ellen," he pleaded. "You don't have to come out but please don't stay in there all night and be cold. Let me give you this blanket to keep you warm."

"Brother Len," Jacob said, "that's not the way a sister should act. It shows a definite erosion of authority in the home situation and in the cultural values of her peer group."

"Sister, she's something else," Rick said, falling into a disdaining dialect. "Brother here is callin' to her, worryin' 'bout her comfort, and she's playin' suicide . . . my my my. . . . Lenard, you should instruct sister in the proper ways of conduct that a sister should observe in your presence and in the presence of your guests."

Len stood red-faced, his hair sprouting atop his head. There was a noise on the far side of the door.

"Lou, if you just open up a little bit I'll give you this blanket so you can keep warm."

"That's right, Lenard, appeal to her reason," Jacob said. "Appeal to her reason. She seems like a reasonable girl." Jacob acted tired of

111

the part he played in the activity so he walked backwards to the couch and nearly sat in the laps of the couple there.

The couple squirmed out of his way and resumed hugging and kissing, but Jacob didn't seem to notice. They leaned farther back, almost lying down, even across Jacob's legs.

The door cracked and a thin brown hand extended. And then Len had the wrist, pulling Lou from the bathroom.

"You dirty mahthafukker!" she screamed when he had her out into the room.

"Now, sister, that isn't the way one should . . ." Rick began.

"Keep out of this, Rick; if you hadn't brought your damned punk cousin in here from the country he wouldn't have fucked up my party."

"Sister's right," Jacob said. "The fault should be shared by more than one."

"Where is that fat bastard?" Lou wanted to know.

"He's gone home with Ceola," someone said.

"Why would she go home with him after he poured beer on her?" she demanded.

"Now, sister . . . the ways of man and woman are . . ." Jacob began.

"Yeah, what goes on behind locked doors ain't . . ." somebody interrupted.

Jacob was in the circle surrounding Lou; the couple on the couch mumbled at being disturbed by the others. Len held Lou's arms and Rick made a speech.

"Now when a man and a woman become . . ."

What's happening? I wondered. And then I knew.

I was back again at the night of the smoker. But there was a difference. Really many differences, but I didn't know most of them then. Rick was speechmaking but there was no laughter. He made similar high-sounding noises as before in the nearly exact voice. In his most precise, clipped, very British accent he arbitrated the issues of the day, handed down the laws, paved the way for peace. But

112

how different the attitude of this group from the others at that lost night of cloaked sex and unaware pantomimed homosexuality.

I looked about. The couple on the couch had stopped fumbling with each other and sat still, listening to Rick's words. Tanya was at his elbow now, her little brown face expressing joy and respect. Lou was quiet, standing counseled, and Len held her gently with a bored expression. The group was quiet, attentive to Rick; the music had been stopped in the back and everyone was in the living room listening to his many words about man and woman and the conduct of each to each, especially and entirely if they were black. He was speaking to them in a weird tongue, one more guise he used that night, and they listened and revered. His trace of earlier speech remained strong enough for him to be known; he was still one of them, he was merely a black boy from the country speaking to other blacks, but he spoke the language of power. How differently this group reacted to his style than those at the smoker. All those white faces had grinned and their breath had snuffled in strained wheezing, and this black group were blank, their masks were exposed and torn away, the look of awe was open in their eyes.

What mask did Rick use to entrance these people? Not the unsuccessful ones he had worn earlier that night. The face of the jester and sport can hypnotize few. But now he was speaking in the same voice, with the same mannerisms, but was it all exactly the same?

No. Not just the same. A hint of mirth at a certain moment when a turn of dialect was made, making a common phrase an absurd pun. A twinkle in his eyes accompanied by a slur to remind all there that night of their low, or rather real, beginnings, a shuffling of feet to mock a half-remembered character, a foolish scratching of the scalp, a "yawhl" exclaimed, zooming in like an idiot's scream and followed by a hesitant triple chuckle of emphasis. No, it wasn't exactly the same as before. But it was a speech nonetheless, and I would never forget it though I didn't hear the words the same as that first night. It wasn't the same but the voice spoke the same, the Queen's English as she had never heard it.

What guise was this? The magician of mood, what part did he play to bring life in that room to a standstill? This was all so new to me. What was it all about; what were Rick and Len and Lou and Jacob and these Black Nationalists and intellectuals about? Just what was *their* game? No one else there seemed surprised or estranged. They all accepted as ordinary this spare, obviously southern negro speaking to them in an imperfect approximation of an Oxford accent. That moment, I believe, was when I became determined to find more about what had happened during that night . . . and since that night, as well as many others, my life has never been the same.

After the speech, Len released Lou and she spun, calling him a foul name and scratching a narrow streak down his cheek. He grabbed her throat and wrestled her to the floor with a strangling hold.

"Now, Len, Len . . ." Jacob pleaded, having hurried from his seat.

"Lenard . . . *brother!* You should know better." Rick hovered over them trying to pull Len off without using force.

I could see that Len wasn't pressing hard, only attempting a convincing scene. Finally, he relaxed and Lou sprang up, snatching the dropped blanket, and with mutters and sobs she raced back into the bathroom and slammed the door. No one tried to get her to return.

"Well, the party's over, brother, so you'll have to go," Rick told me as he had most of the others he had ushered out.

"I'm staying tonight," I said.

"But you have to go when the man wants you out of his house, brother! What sort of statement is that to make?"

"Well, I'm a friend of theirs and they invited me to stay," I said.

He shrugged and pushed out his chest and looked furious when I wouldn't follow his orders.

"Good night," Tanya had said.

I waved at her and caught a flashing glimpse of her brown legs and narrow ankles turning a corner.

Soon most were gone except for Len, who locked himself in the back room; the slim youth, long abandoned by the plump girl, who snored upon the couch, and I, remaining out front. Even Rick had left with pretty Tanya and the rest were gone, whispering what an awful party it had been. The light under the bathroom door snapped off, and I could hear the record player drone softly through the back door.

I stepped out into the darkness of the court to relieve myself of the fullness of the beer, the Southern California sky a starry and smogless expanse above. I drew in a whiff of night air but only filled my chest with the odors of tenements, poverty and the sickness of loneliness. No use thinking that Lou would open the door to me, I thought, any faster than she would to her lover.

He knew he had been dead when they revived him in the intensive care unit, while sewing up his throat without benefit of anesthetics. How he knew and what he knew of his state of being over the past hour he could not describe, ever, but he had just come back from somewhere, he knew, and at that moment in the hospital he felt very very sick.

"When can I talk to him?" said a gray-eyed detective, speaking to the black intern and worried nurse stitching up the six-inch gash in their patient.

"I don't know," replied the surgeon. "He's in bad shape. Lost more blood than most people could and live. I didn't even find his beat for a couple of minutes after those women dragged him in here. . . . Technically, he was a dead man . . . but he's alive now, though not kickin', and you can't talk to him in his shape. We don't know yet, but there could be brain damage from lack of oxygen or shock."

"His eyes are open. Look," said the cop. "Hey, fellah! Hey, buddy! I got to ask you some questions."

"Let him sleep this one off," said the doc. "We don't even know

115

if he can talk yet until the x-rays come back and we find out if his voice box has been damaged or not."

The patient felt more tired than he had ever thought possible, though his eyes caught the slender arm of the nurse move to adjust the plasma above the table, before he slipped again below consciousness.

In three days he was home, his throat bandaged so tightly that he couldn't move his head. But he could whisper. And with his back aching from the stitches there, for he had been stabbed several times in the back, probably when he went into his crouch after being struck in the throat, he surmised.

His mother prayed a lot and nursed him. But his wife didn't come by or call.

His cousin Dinah visited, telling him that her husband Harry was still in the hospital with a punctured spleen, and that Harry had made out the report to the police, so the entire episode was all over now because she and Harry's hospitalization policy could meet their emergency. And his cousin Elvin, Dinah's brother, came by, telling him that he could be proud of himself, he had really put a hurtin' on the punk; Elvin and his boys had heard what had happened that night and went looking for the knifer. They had found and followed his bloodstains ten blocks to the elevated line, where they had disappeared on the crosstown boarding platform. And even his stepfather came by. Both he and his mother hadn't seen him for several years but his aunt Bernell had gotten the word out.

"I don't know what to do with this boy," his mother told his stepfather. "Every time I look around he's being dragged in cut-up or shot-up or beat-up or somethin', that's when he's not bummin' around the world and chasin' any woman that shakes her rear end at him. He's got poor little children to raise and he's acting like Boston Blackie or somebody in the movies." She was proud of her son, nonetheless, for being a known street fighter like his father had been.

"With his luck and the toughness of his head and behind he's bound to be destined for something," his stepfather said.

116

"I pray he's not destined for an early grave," his mother replied.

"It just wasn't your time to go, Stevie," his stepfather told him. "You're part of a greater plan, it seems." His stepfather liked to sound mystical around his mother, especially since she had been frequenting faith healers and spiritualists over the past years.

Several nights later his true father came by. He hadn't seen his father since he was a small boy. His father told his mother and him that he had heard what had happened "through the grapevine," and he pulled a huge revolver and said he was ready to go out with his son, as soon as he got back on his feet, and track down the cowardly dog who had done the deed. His father was thanked properly and told to forget about revenge; "the past is the past," his son said.

His ole man and his mother got drunk after supper and began acting romantic and youngish before they retired to his mother's room, and he never got a chance to talk to his sire. That was the last time he ever saw him.

In two more weeks he was up, and he began carrying his pistol, " 'cause the streets are dangerous."

"Remember, Steven, God has a plan and purpose for you," his mother kept repeating when he went out at night. "Don't fight against your future, son."

It was full day, with the sun burning the streets and courtyard. A dim glow eased under the overhanging balcony of the apartment above Len's place and fell back into the cool corner where I slept. When my eyes opened I saw the slim boy sprawling on the couch and then heard the hiss of the shower in the bathroom. Finally, the boy's snores rumbled through my daze, and I knew that sound had awakened me.

I had made a place to sleep the night before among the pastel leather pillows; I had searched the alcove closet where I saw Len get the blanket he offered Lou, and inside I found an old tattered sheet that I spread upon the grass rug and used to partly cover my arms and chest. The boy on the couch didn't appear to have minded the chill night.

The shower sound stopped and soon Lou stepped out of the bathroom door with her blanket about her like a robe. I shut my eyes, pretending sleep.

"Steve . . . Steve?" she called.

"Yeah," I answered, after a hesitation, and raised myself to my elbows.

She smiled in her horsy way and walked barefooted past me into the kitchen.

"Any coffee?" she called.

I got up and stretched, feeling not too stiff, and walked out behind her.

"Yeah, that sounds great."

"Wait until I put something on," she said in passing, "and I'll get breakfast." She mumbled something in Spanish as she walked by the couch; the boy's snores filled the room.

"Did you sleep well?" she asked when she returned. "Oh, you don't have to do that," she said, seeing me washing the sink-filling dishes.

"I slept great; that grass rug of yours isn't so bad. How did you do?"

She pushed me away from the sink and plunged her small arms up to the elbows.

"Jeezus," she said. "You really like your water hot."

"You get used to it."

She stirred the suds around and rattled a few plates.

"Okay." She smiled. "I'm used to it. I get used to a lot around here. I have to sleep in the bathtub at least once a week around here with that bastard Lenard."

With suds dripping, she pulled her arms from the sink and fixed

118

the coffeepot to perk and opened the refrigerator and counted the eggs.

"How 'bout my special Spanish omelet?" Her voice sounded hollow from the refrigerator.

"Sounds luscious. An old family recipe?"

We smiled a lot that morning; in part, it was from my corny remarks, but more, I believe, was from the night being done and the sun showing us still to be young. The daylight made her squint like a person who works at night; Los Angeles was a poor place for her, I thought. Her creamy complexion would roughen and become swarthy if she wasn't careful. She usually wore her hair in a ponytail but it was knotted that day in a braid.

"Some party," I said.

"I've seen better."

"We both have but it was interesting."

She broke seven eggs in a bowl and began cutting up onion, ham, green pepper and other things over them as I started for the bathroom.

"Get a towel out of the little cupboard in the hallway, Steve," she shouted. "The water's good and hot for a shower, if you want one."

Through the cracked door, I heard her singing among the dishes' clatter. The boy had stopped his sleeping sounds.

Soon I stepped out of the tub and dried. I found a razor in the medicine cabinet and began scraping my stubble.

I thought it strange, my being there in that house, shaving with a borrowed razor. It must be Len's or even Lou's, I mused, for Len showed no signs of ever having shaved. How strange for me to even linger in this part of the world, a place so alien to me. I thought back to the beginning, to my first days in Los Angeles when I hardly knew anyone.

I patted some bay rum on my nicks in Len's bathroom and remembered how long it had been since I had had a car and a good pay check, and how cocky I was when I first hit town, and how often I had dropped out from school. But I had returned to school after every dropout and had gotten my high school diploma from evening school, so that I could better myself, I told myself, then entered college. Now I lived a different life, or thought I did.

The boy on the couch stirred when I came out rubbing the damp towel in my hair. The sun was higher and shining down a hot beam through a slit in the curtains to fall upon his sweating face. I noticed the curtains hanging motionless in the baked air. They were red, the cloth was dyed burlap, and they had been hand-stitched with black thread.

The boy blinked, feeling the sun, and then turned his head away from the brightness; but unable to move out of the heat, he sat up. He groaned and placed a hand upon his head and lay back only to have the sun fall into his eyes once more. Then he dropped his legs over the side of the couch and swung his weight partly over the edge until his knees rested upon the floor and the upper part of his body remained on the couch, stomach down.

"Ohhhh . . ." he said. "Ohhh."

"That sounds like Ernest," Lou said. "Good morning, Ernest," she called.

"Ohhh . . . *goddamn* . . . ohhh, sonnabitch," the boy groaned.

"C'mon, Ernest," Lou called. "Get up from there for your breakfast."

"Ohhh, man . . . you must be out of your head talkin' 'bout breakfast," Ernest said and rolled onto the floor.

"Good morning," I said.

He squinted, his back upon the floor, his head lifted high enough to focus his eyes; he didn't say anything at first, but looked at me intently through muddy eyes.

"Ohhh, now I know it's goin' to be a groovy morning."

Ernest partly crawled, partly staggered into the bathroom, and from the kitchen Lou and I heard his flooding piss spill into the toilet bowl, beyond the open door.

"Want me to call Len?" I asked.

"No, he doesn't get up until the afternoon."

I went back into the front room and took the water-filled tub from the table where the drinks had been served the previous night, and

120

carried the sloshing mess out into the courtyard and dumped the remains down a drain. Inside, I collected beer cans and glasses and ashtrays. Some of the cigarettes had been barely smoked. I pulled these out and pocketed them; the ones with lipstick on them I didn't take. I had promised myself to stop smoking but my mouth felt like the inside of a flannel sock, so I thought nothing could hurt too much. I was pleased I didn't have a real hangover though I hadn't gotten too loaded. As I piled the dirty things on the drainboard and threw the trash in the garbage can, Ernest came sauntering from the bathroom.

"Hey, man, my name's Ernest," he said.

I introduced myself, and offered him one of the scavenged butts.

"Thanks, man. Sorry 'bout that little thing last night, man," he said. "Sometimes I drink a lot and forget that we all have our points of view."

"More my fault than yours. I shouldn't have been butting in."

"What's this all about?" Lou asked.

We took more than ten minutes explaining and by the time we completed our exaggerated versions we were all laughing and I had made a friend of Ernest.

"Yoo hoo, open up, I got my hands full," a voice yelled from outside the door as Lou dished the eggs into our plates.

"Oh, it's Kenyatta," Lou said, excited, and almost dropped the egg pan into the sink. She ran to the kitchen door and opened it. A large tan girl entered holding a gray fluffy cat.

"Kenyatta, baby," Lou said and grabbed the cat from the girl and hugged the animal desperately.

"Well, thanks for nothing," the girl said to her.

"Connie," Lou exclaimed. "Girl, you know I appreciate your keeping Kenyatta." Then, noticing Ernest and me, "I want you to meet a very good friend of mine, Steve, and you know this old bum Ernest," she said, pushing him roughly.

The cat purred and rubbed its head against Lou's breasts. Ernest reached for his plate and I followed his example. Connie declined breakfast and we all went into the living room.

"This sure nuf is good eatin', Miss Lou," Ernest said, in fake dialect.

I sat against the wall on the pillows, Ernest sat next to the console and the girls took the couch. The cat pounced upon the floor, padding over to me, rubbing itself against my legs and purring.

"Don't give that bandit any of your food, Steve," Lou said. "He's an old fake an'll just mess over it."

On the floor next to me was a row of magazines and newspapers. I picked up a magazine with an attractive cover, *The Urbanite;* it had the picture of a beautiful woman on the cover. Her skin was a rich brown that looked velvety and warm. Next to it was a hard-cover book with the name *Horizon,* and it appeared to be a magazine from its contents.

I had never seen these magazines before, and a few of the others I hadn't seen as well; or else only in passing some newsstand had I glanced at their covers, but I had not picked them up or thought of who bought papers like *The People's World* or *Muhammed Speaks.*

At that time I thought myself reasonably familiar with national publications, but I knew nothing of most of these.

The console was opened to the compartment where the record albums were stored in rows, but some were scattered upon the floor where someone had brought them in from the back room. So Len had come out of his room last night and put the records out here, and what else had he done and thought after he saw both me and Ernest stretched out and snoring? Certainly he hadn't knocked at the bathroom door again; surely I wasn't that drunk; I would have heard that much noise; but he had come out of his room, for here were some of the records that had been back there.

I remembered the ones by Oscar Brown, Jr., and Nina Simone but scattered among them were some by someone named Dylan Thomas. I wondered who he was and what instrument he blew. And there were classical records and ones from India on which the musicians played weird instruments with more strings than I could count and there were many African records with pictures on their jackets of tribesmen in native dress beating drums or clicking sticks together. Who listened to all these different records? Could one person enjoy all of them when they were so varied? I couldn't, I knew, and I didn't understand most of that foreign music, for one, and if I did, I convinced myself then, I probably still wouldn't like it.

And what of this entire house I sat in eating an ordinary Spanish omelet? There were pictures upon the walls; strange modern pictures that didn't have any meaning or purpose that I could see, and those that did represent something identifiable were done in such exotic colors and with grotesque patterns and exaggerated forms. The people here looked as strange as some of the pictures upon the walls, but nothing seemed out of place in that house except myself, but I didn't wholly feel that way; in fact, I did fit in though I knew not how.

How did Len and Lou live since neither worked? And who were all their friends, the guys who talked so strangely last night, half educated, part slang and with their black jargon, and the girls with their short haircuts, arching compelling, heavily mascaraed brows and stalking about in rainbow-hued clothes? Why was this all so interesting to me? I had been halfway 'round the world, so then why should I come back to America to find all this, and at the end of a lost continent in Los Angeles? I had read that all the kooks in creation make L.A. at some time; then were Len and his crowd a bunch of exhibitionists and perverts and phonies? I couldn't believe that entirely; at least they knew things, or seemed to. Some of the talk I heard last night, if not overly prejudiced and narrow, was at least intelligent sounding, and was the product of minds capable of rationality. It was so seldom that I encountered intelligence or rationality in Southern California, and for these it was enough for me to find out about this group.

They dressed differently; Lou had on, over her bright leotards, a blouse of the same red burlap as was used for the drapes. Len had worn sandals the times I had seen him and Levi's and groomed a beard and grew his hair wild and woolly. Ernest was dressed like Len and the new girl, Connie, wore a white muumuu and had her short hair bleached brownish orange. And there was Rick to be considered, who was always dressed in a dark suit and many times sported a white bow tie.

123

But I've been around the world, I told myself as I chewed the delicious eggs, savoring the bits of ham, so why should all this bother me after what I had already seen? But I've never seen anything like this before in the States, and never expected to. Is there really a black Bohemia, I wondered, and have I unsuspectingly fallen into it? And why am I accepted by this band? Are their values similar to mine, or do they suspect that I live without the encumbrance of those acquired and intangible attitudes called values, and thus we mutually share bonds of a tested strength—realizing the hollowness of that delusion.

But it's my own fault for being taken by surprise; for the last eight years I have stayed pretty much alone, and away from my people as a group. Part of the time I was out of the country and I knocked around when I got back.

There have always been two main groups of negroes that I have encountered, and I have never fitted into either. There were the higher-ups: the doctors, lawyers, schoolteachers, preachers, petty civil servants, and churchgoers on both levels; and there have been the low-down, or just the people. Both have standards and rules that leave me out, though I am pulled by both poles.

The varied higher levels have all that society crap and family politics and what school one went to and who one's daddy is, and I'm Mr. So-and-so and so that makes you what? The trouble is that when I get in surroundings like that I always open my mouth and explode a bubble of myth or illusion that surrounds their heads, dreams that they must hold to keep their delusions of place and rank, and then I am reported for being a destroyer of ignorance, though they find other names than that, and I am reclassified and reshuffled to find myself ejected from their enclaves.

I once had a friend that I had met in a private high school in Philly. He invited me to his home in the suburbs. He called the school we attended a prep school but I never thought of it as being any more than a high school in which its students paid tuition, unlike public schools. There weren't even residence facilities. I don't know what his folks did but they lived in a large white house in one of the few suburbs surrounding Philadelphia available for negroes then. I had just gotten back from Europe the month before, and during the evening his mother and sister began questioning me about my experiences abroad. The old lady kept trying to compare my screwing around the countryside with her guided tours, and the girl had been "on the Continent" (as they called it) four times before she turned eighteen.

We had been drinking from the private bar that they took a lot of pride in and as I drink more than I should whenever I am insecure, I had a bit of a load on. They kept questioning me. Asking me the most stupid questions, like how did I find my treatment by whites in Europe in comparison to those in the United States (as if there were other than whites there to their way of thinking as the Europeans wished them to). I should have told them that the only Europeans that I had ever met had been whites; all the dark souls that I had encountered anywhere on this earth and known have been previously identified and categorized as coming from Jamaica or Africa or India or the Islands (wherever that is) or america, that is, if I wasn't standing upon the soil of america at the time. Those with dark skins born in white lands were referred to as mulattoes or quadroons or octoroons or Moorish or something else to shift the blame for their being found black outside of a black land, even though they were to me Europeans, at least in their minds. What a confusion there that evening in that Pennsylvania *colored* heaven, with all the Scotch and the smiles of my buddy's juicy little sister who went to a private school "nearly" on the Main Line. I thought all types of things: of how everything changed all the time as one moved about, how in England I found something, in France some difference in a look-alike situation, and in Italy, Greece, Spain, Turkey and North Africa I found others. But no matter where I traveled I was an american *there*, so long as I remained outside of america, even while the black Europeans were not "true" Europeans. And there lies the catch word. True. Or maybe "authentic" would be closer. The European's excuse is that darkies in their lands aren't indigenous, but how do white americans make themselves the sole americans when blacks are the *soul* americans? It is certain to be the product of force.

What ironies. Here in america I am always a negro and all other blacks and browns in the world to americans are "Them thar god-damn foreign niggers." I am never an american until I step out of america, and I have found negroes in no other locales than american minds and newspapers. Even americans are not accepted for them-selves in any corner of the earth. My existing as but an abstraction leaves me less than even a lowly white man, or else a figment as immense as the truth.

It was so confusing and that family of well-tended women thought they were teasing me by asking about the women I had met and if I found foreign girls prejudiced, and there I was blabbing to those black virginal-minded females who thought they were really ameri-cans that the color of american money is all most of the women I had met could see in me, at least the few I could afford. That didn't go over too big and the vibrations began getting jerky and I took more drinks 'cause nobody was talking much then and I later woke up being pushed from my friend's car in front of my door and he said I had been insulting by vomiting on his mother's imported rug. And I asked him where had it been imported from, but he screeched off leaving me thinking that I had puked and so what. I planned to pay the cleaning bill.

He didn't speak to me after that and spread rumors around school about me like I thought I was too worldly to be in his fraternity. He knew I was too old to go for that little-boy stuff of paddles and demerits and such nonsense. That's why we had become friends at first. I was older than he and seemed interesting to him for doing things he hadn't. It's just as well we fell out, for I would have never fitted into his group. If things had not ended that night they would have surely when I had done something worse to his way of thinking.

And then there's the people on the lower end, who I get along with much better—the dispossessed, the poor and black, the thieves, pimps, artists, whores and street people, my spiritual brothers and

126

sisters—get along with fine except that I open my mouth and try and enlighten them, and then they think that I'm a wise guy or I've been to school or have prospects or something stupid like that and if we don't get in a fight right then they are suddenly scheming on me for what they think I have or will certainly get or else are putting me down for being "above" them. "Who the hell you think you are to be enlightening somebody?" they all seem silently to scream.

So as far as I go with my people, blacks as a whole, I hang somewhere in social limbo. I have never learned to be cool and have just enough sense to not be completely square. I am just here, I guess, or so I thought until I met Len and his crowd.

With my toast I mopped the last of the eggs up and swallowed it, washing it down with coffee.

"That sho tastes like mo'," Ernest said.

"That better hold you till supper," Lou replied.

The girls had been talking of Rick. Connie was very interested in his whereabouts and how the party had turned out.

Lou gave her version of how she suffered at the hands of Len.

"Even before it began Lenard started fukkin' up by invitin' that Tanya," she said.

"You mean Tanya Jefferson?" Connie asked.

"Yeah; he should know that that little bitch is just out to make trouble," she said. "I sure wish you were here, girl."

"Joe won't let me out Saturday nights. Dammit!"

Ernest walked past me, taking his plate out to the kitchen, and returned with the hardly touched wine jug and glasses. He made another trip to get more glasses and began pouring.

"Up to the lips and down it slips. Look out, stomach, here it comes." He made his toast and we swallowed together.

"That little cousin of Rick's is a big drag," Lou said.

"Yeah, I told Rick that boy would get him in trouble," Connie replied. "He's too young. Should'a stayed in Maryland."

Ernest pulled a Miles Davis record out of the stack and put it on the turntable. He sat back on the floor and we drank wine and listened to Miles and refilled our glasses and discovered that we were together in our mutual comradeship. I was secure and more comfortable there than I would have been in my own small room.

He raped her twice—two separate times her black face stared up at him in drunken disbelief—with at least a year separating the episodes.

They were among his best rapes—quick and clean—and some of the more satisfying, and little guilt was attached to them, except that vague guilt he felt for not feeling guilty of being a rapist. That guilt that nibbled at him, that special type of small, nibbling guilt, those numerous and distinct tiny tears in his sanity, from not suffering like he had supposed other men are to suffer privately for their wanton acts.

His seat was in front of Jess's, and he didn't know him, didn't even remember seeing Jess before that day Jess threatened him. He had leaned his elbow back on Jess's desk, not conscious of the movement in his moment of leisure, as he was daydreaming about seducing a neighbor's daughter, as he did so much then and afterward, and Jess shoved his elbow, hurting the not yet healed scrape.

"Get yo scabby ole diseased arm offa my desk!"

He turned and glanced at Jess from the corners of his eyes.

128

"You don't like it? You want ta make somethin' out of it with that ole nasty syph arm of yours?"

He swung back toward the front and reached for his school-issued pen and dipped it in the fountain of black water-thinned ink and began scratching out the seventh-grade lesson.

"That's right, you better keep those big booby eyes of yours where they belong . . . with that old syphy arm."

It's not syphy, he thought. Doesn't even look syphy. It was an accident.

In the last hot days of August Homer and he rode their bikes farther and farther from Derby Street. Homer seemed to know most of the new territory; he and Ray Crawford must have explored this territory last spring before Ray disappeared into the South, thought Chuck, for Homer led the way with his strong, certain pedaling and fancy twitching of his bike's rear end, to make the fox tail tied there float out like an enormous fuzzy flower, dead too soon as a preview to autumn.

They were in a part of Willow Park that Chuck had not seen before, and after pedaling about a mile along a bridle path, beside the creek, Homer turned across a small high-arched bridge that straddled the creek. Almost immediately they had to get off their bikes and begin rolling them up a steep trail which wound up the forest-hidden hillside. In about fifteen minutes they reached the top and panted for breath in the pine grove they found there.

"See across there, Chuck? That's ah golf course. And down ah ways is a highway and a giant bridge where you can look down on where we just come from. Way down so the creek and the road look like they're made for kids."

"Let's go down the road, Homer! Let's go!"

"Nawh. Nawh, we came up here so we could ride back down fast as hell."

"Yeah, let's go down the trail . . . c'mon!"

As they started, "Ya know what I call this trail we just climbed, Chuck? . . . Deadman's Trail!"

129

And the two climbed back on their bikes and started on the fast trip down, but with the bottom in sight, after he had careened around the last twist in the path, Chuck lost control and crashed into the railing and he and his bike rolled and tumbled behind Homer's speeding wheels and frenzied fox tail to the exact foot of the small bridge.

When Chuck's eyes opened he saw the other bridge, the gigantic bridge, almost directly above him, with Homer's head framed in one of its great arches, grinning down at him like a black moon.

"Heee heee . . . you sho looked funny rollin' like a big ball down that mountain," Homer had said for years afterwards. "And Jesus . . . I couldn't figger where all that blood was comin' from, Chuck. Gawd! You looked like a muddy ball of blood and all . . . hee hee . . . all dirty . . . heee heee . . . but you sure did look funny rollin' down that hill behind me. I damn near broke mah ass tryin' to see you in my rear-view mirror and not break mah ass too."

"I was in a bike accident at Willow Park an' skinned myself up."
"You got syph . . . don't lie to me, boy."
"I'm not lyin'. . . ."
"Y'are!"
"Nawh, I'm not!"
"You callin' me a liar?"
"Yeah, if you say I got that stuff."
"You think you're smart, don't you? You little liar."
"I'm not lyin'."
"Y'are!"
"I'm not!"
"Y'are too!"
"No, I'm not. . . . Hey . . ."
The teacher noticed them. "You, Steven Benson . . . and Jess Simpson . . . I want you to stop that chattering."
"What'chou want?" Jess asked Chuck, before they slipped down into their seats and tucked their attentive heads over their lessons.
"What's syph?" Chuck asked.

And that's how Jess and Chuck met. They became friends almost immediately. Mainly because Jess knew so many things that Chuck didn't. Chuck could use him so he had to make friends with Jess. For Jess loved to talk and brag and lie, for hours, and he showed Chuck how to do things like play poker and inhale cigarette smoke and how to get old winos to go into the liquor store for them if they offered the drunkies a swig out of the bottle.

That was a few of the things that Jess taught Chuck. Jess was from a big family. His mother was always or seemed always pregnant. Pregnant and cheerful, that's how he knew her.

The afternoon of the arm incident, Chuck was invited to Jess's home. And he accepted. They traveled together up Eighth Street, Jess's long legs stalking off the blocks and his arms flapping as he lied and laughed with Chuck, finding out what he could about Chuck so he could use it later for some put-down or the dozens game. It was a cold October day, the sky dingy and low, and they knew it was going to rain.

When Jess pushed in the door to his apartment a smell assaulted Chuck that he tried not to show that he noticed. It was a smell that he had encountered before, from his aunt's home with the five sisters and brothers—his favorite cousins—and, sometimes, himself, and from a family named Johnson, new from Mississippi, who lived on his street, Derby Street, or at least their back yard fronted on that side street, and Chuck frequently tried to squeeze the breasts of the big-legged yellow girls in the family, while the brothers ran like scared hares as the girls fought like amazons for their honor and virginity, as if they fought for their entire tribe, but their houses—Jess's, Chuck's aunt's and cousins' and the Johnsons' of Mississippi—stunk commonly, from age, baby shit, not enough soap, rats, cheap roach destroyer and sweat. Also, from collard greens, bleach, chicken fried in fish grease, Pine Oil disinfectant, pigs' feet, ninety-nine-cent perfume, conk, and what have you in funktown.

Jess's family was mainly made up of girls, at least the older children, of which Jess was third oldest, being there was a sister already

131

married and in Harlem, and then there was Diane and then Jess and next Debra and on and on with boys appearing randomly until there were more than twelve sisters and brothers in all, with the mother still becoming pregnant yearly, making the family seem predominantly female.

The father, Jessie, Sr., was tall and angular as his son Jess. A bit of a raconteur and too blasé for someone with so much family, at least in Chuck's opinion, and somewhere mixed up in it all—the Simpson family—was a granddad and grandmom who never said much separately or together when Chuck was around except to mutter, but were known from reports dropped in Jess's incessant yammering to have argued bitterly and long, criticizing everything and -one, including Jesus and the virgin birth.

Into this scene Chuck came and was handed a fried egg sandwich after telling Jess's mother that his own mother didn't get home from work for another several hours and it was all right to stay over and to play and hang out in general.

"Good . . . we can go over to see Vivian and Delores," Jess said. Which he and Chuck did.

Vivian was supposed to be Jess's girl in a sort of loose way, and Delores was Vivian's cousin that, and not too secretly, Jess wanted for his girl. She was black, that Delores was; black and beautiful as only a really pretty black girl can be, with white white eyes and shiny shiny teeth which smiled and smiled at Chuck.

And Chuck fell in love, meaning, in an unconscious way, he wanted to give her a baby.

The girls lived with an alcoholic aunt who wouldn't let the boys in, but they called to the cousins through their window and soon the pair were outside with them, all their breaths panting out steam, and they giggling and laughing, acting frisky.

Jess tried to kiss Delores; Vivian got mad, spit at him and called Jess "You ole black dawg!"

The aunt saw and heard the incident, as she was peeping bleary-eyed around the parlor curtain, and the girls had to go in.

132

So Chuck went home, Jess following, and they cooked a huge omelet and played records and Chuck telephoned next door to see if Homer was home, or Homer's sisters. Homer wasn't at home, and his sisters, Dora and Marigold, were staying in their small rooms in their small house next door. And Chuck's mother came home, introducing herself to Jess and fixing them all a good dinner with meat, a leafy green vegetable, a starch, milk and lemonade, and a not too heavy or rich dessert, maybe jello.

Then Jess left for home after watching television for three or four hours or so.

"Who's that long lanky yellow nigger, Chuck?" Homer asked, after Jess had been coming by for a week.

"Just a guy from school."

"What's he always down here for? Ain't he got no home?"

"Sure, but we're in the same class. . . . Besides, he's got a nice-lookin' sister."

Homer wanted to know who Jess's sister was. Chuck told him about Diane; she was the prettiest and nearly Homer's age. Homer wanted to know if he could meet her. Chuck planned to invite her down with Jess, Vivian and Delores and have a party. It was set for Friday night.

Friday night Jess came first as he always did, saying that the girls would be along soon and who the hell was this Homer guy who wanted to meet his sister. Chuck tried to cool him for he knew Homer would be over soon, and Chuck didn't want to have the evening start off badly by Homer, who was from South Carolina, busting Jess in the mouth, which was what Homer was hoping to do, as Homer didn't generally mix well.

Chuck was anxious to see Delores. They had been getting closer. He took her to the movies every Saturday afternoon, not alone, for Jess would somehow come along, with his giggles, raucous chomping of popcorn, and his wanting to put his arm around Delores. He

133

tried to share the black girl's kisses with Chuck, wished and attempted to feel her special, private places that only Chuck was allowed; and afterwards, all during the week, he hoped to be Chuck's confidant to learn of those secret moments of Chuck's and Delores's in her hallway that he was barred from, as well as being Delores's conveyer of intimate news to Chuck. He gossiped as much as any girl.

They were nearly inseparable, that trio. Vivian stopped seeing Jess but he told Chuck that he still snuck over to her hallway and did lewd things to the skinny girl while her aunt snored in drunkenness. And Vivian was a friend of some of Jess's sisters, and the things that were purported to have gone on over at Jess's own house between him and Vivian, when she visited, under the collective noses of his grandparents, parents and his dozen or so sisters and brothers, were difficult for Chuck to believe.

That night they partied; Chuck's mother excused herself to visit or date or whatnot, and Chuck and his friends drank and had a fight, which was not that at all.

Diane came in radiant, leading Delores, Vivian, a younger sister, Dollface, and some other girl that nobody knew but who had strong B. O. and halitosis, though a nice smile. Homer's sisters came over and a couple of guys from up the block came down, Horsey Burton and Fat Boy. There were more girls than guys so the guys were glad, but most could not dance.

Chuck played host and drank not as much as the others, for it was his house, and he wanted to make a good impression on Delores; besides, Homer's sister Marigold had promised to punch Delores in the mouth because she (Delores) was an "ole black hussy who thought she was better than anybody else." Also, Chuck didn't want Jess or Homer to get too close to Delores, so he was sober to a fault.

Diane, Jess's sister, was about five six, slim and more yellow than Jess. Her cheeks grew pink from the weather and she had bangs which she called Chinese. She was the favorite in her family, dressed better and was sent across town to a school that the other kids didn't get to go to. She was bright and witty as well as pretty, and married an up 'n' comin' prize fighter a few years later who was nearly blinded in a fight with Sugar Ray Robinson and quickly retired to jobs as noted negro auto salesman, liquor salesman, Florsheim shoe salesman, Hart Schaffner & Marx suit salesman, bartender and pawnshop clerk. The couple moved to New York, only to return in periodic swirls of glamour, with whiffs of the Big Apple trailing from their three-year-old Cadillac's exhaust.

Vivian came in like the slinky predatory lynx she was. She had a narrow, wicked face that gave males instant erections, and was born knowing what her sex should know, and many were the times Chuck had wished that he hadn't gotten wrapped up with Delores. Vivian and Homer hit it off from the first, being that they were both no-nonsense types, though Homer made occasional bumbling overtures to Diane and Delores, who were having a good time and not allowing themselves to become charmed by Homer's country ways.

Dora, Homer's older sister, was silent, strong and black. She had a proud, stern appearance which was often mistaken for primness. But Chuck did something to her he called "dry fuckin' " during their lights-way-down-low parties and in her hallway when he visited Homer when her parents were out, and when she had a yen or hankerin' for moving her exciting, hard body against his. And she married early for the usual reasons for early marriages, some anonymous-looking young brown-skinned fellow who none of the neighborhood knew or had heard of before, or could remember after the newlyweds had moved to Chester, Pennsylvania, where he worked on the riverfront or in the train yards or somewhere, and he was only referred to thereafter as "Dora's husband."

Marigold was there. Marigold—big, loud, blowsy, pretentious and stupid, Homer's and Dora's sister. She was there seeking Chuck.

Delores's bright eyes shone and her short hair was curled and burnt by hot combs to expose her scalp for the festivities.

"After Hours," a sort of slow-grind nasty-nasty record, was played most of the night, and they all danced with the lights way down low, those danced who could, and once even with the lights out, until Marigold began bellowing about how they should be turned on, though nobody had tried to dance with Marigold for half an hour.

So there they were. On the small street in late winter or early spring with the sky wet and the old buildings crumbling and paint flaked, the fences wooden, the street lights dim and glowing.

And Marigold slapped Chuck in the face, in a corner, and said, "You think you so smart, Stevie Benson. . . . If Ray Crawford were back you wouldn't even see me. We'd probably be at the movies right now!"

"Ray Crawford never even looked at you, girl. Stop lyin'!"

"You think you smart, Chuckie. . . . You just wait till Ray gets back, you ole black nigger!"

And they partied on into the night on back street U.S.A.

The apartment units were off the street. Like a black stopped-up river, the street flowed south moving a current of vehicles along in a jam, packed so close they threatened to collide and spill onto the curbs. Behind a tailor shop and through a narrow grease-slickened driveway the court opened out into a dreary lot between two apartment houses. There were eight apartments in the smaller units, four on the ground floor and four upstairs, with stairs outside running upwards to a balcony where no one ever stood. The walls in these apartments were thin enough for neighbors on each side to hear an occupant's movements, but most crouched in their rooms making few noises, though a close listener could detect breathing when anyone was at home.

None of the tenants knew one another. When one was leaving the building he would first spy out of the curtains and between the blinds to see that all his neighbors were inside and then he would slip from his door and steal to the parking area in back, if he owned an auto, and attempt to reach the street without being seen. When one apartment dweller returned and inadvertently met another slipping from the building, the two would find interest in the sky or ground or in the cracked peeling brown walls of the small stucco building where they lived. Being too close to hide, they would throw up their hands in gestures of fondness and community spirit.

The rear exit of the larger apartment faced the courtyard of the smaller units. No one had ever been seen entering or leaving this building by that exit, though there were over thirty apartments in it and there were curtains in the windows that flapped each night when hands lifted the windows, and sounds, unlike in the smaller units, flowed onto the court at the dinner hours.

During the day the Southern California sun baked the court, but no children regretted the lack of grass or even were present to doodle on the crumbling cement of the court with the grease drippings from the autos, and even cats avoided this stretch, preferring to seek out baked dirt back lawns on near side streets, or to remain at home.

Len's neighbors ignored his noise; they also ignored the man in the end apartment who punched his wife in the face each weekend, setting her to scream and weep in the late afternoons as the smog-coated sun swallowed the sky.

There were two entrances to Len's apartment on the court side, and another which opened out on a fence so close that garbage cans could not be stored. One court entrance opened upon the living room and the other upon the kitchen, but all three entrances seemed back exits from other places.

Len came out of his room around two. We were lying in the living room. I had been napping upon the pillows where I had lain all day. Connie was on the couch where she had stretched out after her first glass of wine. Ernest and Lou were in different areas of the floor. A jazz program played on the radio and the sun had slipped past the window behind the apartment across the court.

"Well, people, how are you?" Len said, smiling at us all.

He had on a shirt; its long tails hung down close to his knees. His hair stood about his head like a wiry nest and he squinted without his glasses.

"Hey, man, what's happenin'?" Ernest asked.

"Hello," Connie greeted. "You're lookin' good, brother."

Len grinned more. I waved a drowsy salute. Lou turned her head away, and he, seeing the cat beside her, walked over and bent down and petted it.

"How's Kenyatta, how's the old pussy?"

"He don't need you pattin' on him," Lou said, pushing his hand from the animal. "He knows you don't like him."

Len bent forward and kissed her on her turned cheek and she flushed, holding his hand tight now and twisting her head for his waiting tongue. His back was turned to me and his bending pulled his shirt tail high. After the first glimpse of his brown bottom with the hairs curling out of its recesses, I shut my eyes.

"Go on, Lenard," I heard Connie say. "Do the thing, brother!" was the last I heard as I fell asleep.

I awoke to Lou's shrill laughter in the bathroom and the sound of splashing water. Len's voice mumbled among her squeals and Connie read a book on the couch. Ernest lay upon his back, a pillow under his head, and blew out cigarette smoke in spewing clouds.

Len came out of the bathroom later dressed in Levi's, sandals and the same red shirt he had on before. He walked to the console and began fiddling with the dials.

"I'd like you folks to hear something," he said when he stopped the record.

A reserved voice came from the radio.

"This is your listener-sponsored station . . ." the voice said.

Lou came from the bathroom with a towel about her head and a pink flush on her smile.

"Shit, Lenard," she said. "I don't want to listen to that intellectual shit all afternoon."

"Please, Lou Ellen," he replied. "We have guests and there is an

African affairs program coming on soon that I think everyone would like to hear."

"Well, why didn't you say so?"

She found a place among me and Ernest and the cat. Len sat near her head.

"Well, how do you feel, Steve?" Len said when he saw my eyes open.

"Pretty good."

"And now we shall resume our afternoon program of Gregorian chants . . ." the radio announcer said.

"That's all we need," Ernest grumbled and shifted himself and crawled to the wine jug.

"Where's the African program, Lenard?" Connie asked.

"Yeah, why the hell we gotta lissen to that shit?" Lou questioned.

"This very fine music will be off in an hour and then we can all listen to the African program," Len said.

"Mahthafukker!"

Before Ernest capped the jug Lou asked him to refill her glass.

"Lou," Len said. "Don't you think you've had enough?"

"Sheet, if I have to hear that shit on'na radio I might as well enjoy myself."

"Yas, ma'm, Miss Lou." Ernest kidded. "Anything yawhl say."

Len darkened a bit and turned to me.

"I hear you draw some, Steve," he said.

"Give me a cigarette, Connie," Lou said.

"Damned, you're not going to smoke too?" Len said, twisting his head to hers.

She reached out for the cigarette Connie offered. "Thanks," she said, picking up Ernest's matches.

"That's a very bad sight," Len said, "to see a woman with one of those foul things hanging out of her mouth."

Lou blew her first breath of smoke into his face.

He turned to me again. "I hear that you write some too."

"I only play around with a little poetry."

"That's fine; who do you like writing today?"

I could not answer. Who were my favorite authors? I could have told him some I had liked before coming to college, but I didn't want him to know how unread I was, if he didn't know already, and I would not name a writer that every college freshman must read, for that would have suggested that I knew too few.

I had started writing doggerel and verse years before in my teens, and had resumed when I began college. I was reading so much more since beginning college the summer before, and books I would have never known of otherwise. New to me were *1984, Brave New World, The Pearl,* which I had missed when reading Steinbeck earlier, and there were many others. There were inexpressible feelings inside me that my new reading had brought to the surface. With my poetry and drawings I tried to explain and smooth out my emotions. I felt trapped for the first time in life since beginning college, even though I walked outside of barred windows and guarded institutions that made confinement actual, but no more concrete; I felt trapped for the first time by my skin and by my lacks that I had never known of before. For a sense of freedom I wrote pages about trees, the moon and stars, reality, time, existence, death, and love, the unfound and hopeless love that I believed I had lost. I feared to show this part of me, but I did press a few pages on some people.

It was a scorching afternoon one summer when I sat in the nearly empty school patio with the blond girl reading my poems. She looked up at a shadow passing in the sunlight and waved and called Len over. I was annoyed that she became that easily distracted from my poems but I kept silent; Len stood there in an outfit of sandals and boating trousers that resembled pedal pushers, wearing a boat-neck shirt and a beard and the most hair worn by any man I had ever seen. He and the girl had a brief conversation about some test they both said they did poorly on and then she handed Len my poems, introducing me as their author. She made a few pleasant and meaningless comments about the work, and I felt it made up for her rudeness.

"Oh, you write?" Len had commented.

140

He had looked at the poems and spent more than half an hour telling me what he thought was good in them and what bad. The girl finally left, swinging her grass bag and showing her firm ankles as she turned the corner, but he stayed, explaining things about images and rhythms, things I didn't know about. He invited me down to his house; I couldn't go that afternoon, but I went the following weekend. He and Lou were on their way out somewhere so we only drank a cup of tea and then school was over for the summer the next week, so we didn't meet again until I called him the day of the beach party.

"This is called 'Liberal Jewish White Girl,' " Len said, after I couldn't tell him what writers I liked best.

He had told me he wrote also and I had asked to see his work. Lou groaned when he announced the title and Ernest gave a snort.

" 'Me, son of Ham, the white-black nigger hiding behind a flesh-colored band-aid lie,' " he began.

It was an essay about how the left-wing seduces negro boys to their cause by introducing them to white girls and encouraging "miscegenation," as Len called it. I could tell there was a lot of autobiographical material in the piece, so I didn't question its validity.

He spoke of black intellectuals in a historical context.

" 'Before me was Richard Wright, Du Bois . . .' " he continued.

He read off the names of negroes I had read about, negroes I had heard of briefly. It was like returning to a place that I had abandoned once, a place of my childhood that I longed for but feared. Marcus Garvey, Frederick Douglass. Names from history and modern personalities spilled from the pages, all connected by the color of the characters' black skins and the dark history that they influenced. Len had his name intermingled with theirs, but where did I stand?

What was he speaking of? I wondered. Abolitionists. There was no need to mention their names in these times. History was fine to know, I thought as he read the essay, but history died with the individuals who made it. Then he turned to politics, economics and society, subjects I had never thought of in relation to color.

What was the link between the left wing, the white left wing that he spoke of, and the blacks, as well as militant negroes? I knew he was sympathetic to militancy, so how could he be or have been so involved with the left wing as to have gone to bed with their women and been in love with some, as he said? I was confused. If the white left wing is liberal to negroes, then how could militant blacks be part of it? Militancy was against whites. Didn't I know? Hadn't I heard the speeches on the corners of Harlem and Philly years before, so how could the whites, who were the *enemies* and would someday be cast in the pit during the great war that the militants prophesied between blacks and whites, be on the same side?

Could there be different types of black militants; could Black Nationalism have differences, divisions and factions? And could whites be so different in their politics? Yes, I knew there were the Democrats and the Republicans, but there was also something called the left wing, which both these groups thought was poison. I was naïve and knew it. I wanted to learn but I didn't want to rush in too fast. I guess new ideas have always been the most difficult diet for me to digest.

"Wow, that's pretty good, Lenard," Connie said after he was through. "You've made some changes since I last heard it, haven't you?"

"Yes," Len said. "I've tightened it up."

"Liberal Jewish white girls, sheeet," Lou said. "If they messed with you they musta been liberal."

The wine was getting low and as I filled my glass again, Ernest reached for the jug, chuckling at Lou's remark.

"Here is a haiku that I did for Lou," Len said.

I asked him what a haiku was. He is one of those persons who take pleasure in explaining things that another person doesn't know or understand. I believe that he even went out of his way to find things of interest that his friends and guests wouldn't know about.

"Oh, the haiku is a Japanese form of poetry with seventeen . . ."

He told me the structure of the poem and a little of its history. Of how the Japanese court had used it centuries before as some sort of

142

game and all that type of thing. His haiku was about Lou's tears dropping from her nose. That was about all, just that, and he was very pleased with it and she didn't curse quite as hard when he read it the second time.

In all the time I knew them while they were together, I never saw them kiss except once. They were continually arguing or pouting or making up, but except for that one time over the cat, my memories of them together were without a kiss or other sign of obvious affection. I knew that they had strong feelings for one another, though I couldn't call it love, for it is a bit more than I would take upon myself, saying who was in love and who was not. I believe that I came in on the tail end of something in both of their lives, and as a friendly observer my connection would not allow me to be objective.

Then Len read me other poems, pretty good ones, I thought, and he began suggesting things for me to read. He had a lot of books. Mostly all types, though not much science, which I wouldn't be too interested in except biology and psychology. He had books of history, of English grammar and lit; of journalism, and a lot more. He suggested that I read some modern poets. Cummings and Eliot, and Ginsberg, whom I had heard of and had read *Howl,* and Ferlinghetti. He gave me mimeo magazines with names like *Floating Bear* and *Wild Dog,* and then began on novels, pointing out *The Invisible Man* by Ralph Ellison.

I remember when I was in boot camp in the navy, all of seventeen, and I had bought the same book in the PX. I began reading it and since I've always read a lot, I kept through its pages until past a hundred. And I didn't know what I had read. I laid the book aside because it was unimportant whether I finished it then. I was annoyed; I didn't know what I was reading. I couldn't handle it. I had just finished reading the entire series of Mickey Spillane books, and I wanted a change. In fact, I changed my tastes a lot in the next four years. Before I got out of the navy I had read *The Organization Man, The Theory of the Leisure Class* and, most important, *The Black Bourgeoisie,* by E. Franklin Frazier. But I never got back to Ellison for years.

"Have you read Richard Wright, Steve?" Len asked.

I nodded and told him I had read some of Wright, and he asked me what works. I told him. He didn't know that I was trembling inside.

I had learned to read early. When many of the other kids were outside playing ball or swinging on the playground swings, before the time of TV, I was usually curled up with a book. Of course, I played ball and romped with my succession of dogs and skated, but I also read, and reading took the place a lot of the time of building model airplanes or doing what other seven- or eight-year-olds do. The first book my mother gave me was *Black Boy.*

She had always read to me until I had gotten too big and then she began getting me books from the library, but *Black Boy* was the first book she bought particularly for me. She hardly ever told me about the world, about what to look for in life unless it was a part of her vision of the future. I guess her ways were to be a protection for me, but the only thing I think it has really done is have me disbelieve in the dreams of futures. Whenever I grew old enough to be made aware of something, like sex or that I am a negro and would be treated differently from other people, she left me a book on my night table. And so she gave me *Black Boy,* to enlighten me. My life has held recurrences of that horrible experience ever since.

After I had read that autobiography of Richard Wright, I had been physically unable to read another negro author for over ten years, but she never knew, and I didn't even admit the fact to myself. I had just refused to believe there were any other negro writers and that made it unnecessary even accidentally to relive the trauma. I even stopped reading harmless Frank Yerby when I found he was negro and refused until my late teens to read books with negro themes and subjects. It was frightening to believe an autobiography, but I believed literally in the characters in books then and in their situations, and the monstrous life that Wright portrayed in that book could as well have been *mine:* this is the fear I screamed of at night. In all my reading until then and most of it since, except for Whitman, that was the single character that I felt a definite spiritual kinship with, and I attempted to strangle that apparition's first breath. My hands are still partially encircling its black throat.

The description of his white-looking grandmother was like those I had heard of some of my distant relatives. And I did have a very fair aunt with long stringy hair who was old enough to be a grandmother and the entire similarity scared me more thoroughly than all the promised damnations of hell in the Bible. I do not understand why I compared that experience of reading *Black Boy* to cringing under the denunciations of the ancient prophets and fearing for the immortal everlasting soul I believed in then, but reading that book I somehow feared for myself as I have few times since. It can't be this way, I believe my child's mind reasoned; I won't believe it's like this. I don't live like this. No one does, at least no one I know, so what is he saying these things for? What is he doing? Why is he trying to destroy me? With all my will I fought the accusations of living in a false world of childhood and adolescent comfort and smugness, but I knew he spoke the truth, that things he described in such brutal detail did really happen—only in a different place. I could not believe that such things confronted me. Down south, that's it, I reasoned, down south, for I had heard of "down home" numerous occasions through tales, jest and table talk of the elders, though I could not imagine where the "country" was, or if it was actually a real place, or illusionary like the story lands of ghosts and witches and trolls. I never knew until much later that I was already and soon would be even more acquainted with the South, and would have such a fear and hate instilled in me for "down home" that even today it is vital for me to be objective and not allow prejudice to infect my feelings when I meet someone with a hard southern accent—whether they be black or white.

Actually most of my newer friends were recently arrived from "down home"; but from the way in which they spoke of the land they fled, it was a distant wonderland of sights and smells and adventures, far superior and unlike the then fabulous New Jersey farm of my nearly white aunt. They must lie, I felt. I *knew* they lied and I secretly hated them the more for their trying to deceive me. My new friends from the South acted differently, so strange and awkward their first long years in the city and not like myself, who knew the city's ways . . . I thought. And some never have changed.

I wasn't afraid to speak to whites or shy in their presence like many of my friends were; no, I went to school with whites every day and would punch one in the mouth if he wasn't my friend or had gotten out of line. I even walked Sylvia Greenglass home each day of my next to last year in elementary school, carrying her books and sometimes staying late at her house for hot creamy chocolate that her mother fixed on chill days. Sylvia with the auburn hair and pink cheeks and ears that brightened crimson in the wintertime. I think of that day when I walked her home and my friends from school threw snowballs at us; and Sylvia and I laughed and trotted along, with me stooping in the cold, scooping up the icy whiteness and returning their volleys up Seventh Street, yelling and panting out clouds of steam until one of the snowballs hit Sylvia's ear. The moment froze as if it were etched by icicles to freeze my heart's hammering. Then Sylvia and I hurried the last six blocks to her house as she cried, with me knowing that it was an awful accident which found me helpless after the damage was done, but I whispered to myself that I could have prevented it by being nearer her, warding off the balls of snow and ice. I couldn't explain to Mrs. Greenglass when she opened the door; Sylvia stood there on the steps, whimpering and sputtering about her ear, and I begged forgiveness as if I had made the little pink girl my target. Her mother did not invite me in that afternoon, nor any other, and Sylvia stopped playing with me at recess nor would she allow me to walk her home again. I hated the ones who threw at us that afternoon, hated them for causing the trouble, but they were my friends, Brother and Timmy, the other two negroes in the school. We called ourselves "colored" in those days.

I hated my first two friends for parting me from a white girl; the contest today is being probably still played with the same results. Brother had a soft southern accent and had been in the city for only a couple of years but he knew more things about the streets and how its people acted than I did. We remained friends for over ten years but to me he was always a southern negro, and so not really my friend. Timmy was from a family with a lot of kids and his big brothers always threatened to beat me up and take my possessions until I got big enough not to take threats from anyone. To me I seemed long in getting that big, but the day came when I couldn't allow any more slights to go unchallenged, and during the course of those years I have lost all those friends of then, through the blood, rage and battles within our ignorance and coming manhood, and no others have I hated so much nor have I met since any that have entirely replaced them.

It has always been too easy for me to take up with the white world; it has always been too easy to find some sort of acceptance for me from whites. Somehow I had learned to speak in a close approximation to their way; my reading had conditioned me to search in the world for many of their values. We had gone to the same schools, with my being for the first six years the single negro in my classes and always near the top. That type of conditioning is murderous to throw off at once, it is subtle and almost sure in most cases to twist a black soul into a hybrid freak of some kind; it lulls the victim into refusing to see the darker aspects of the world. It gives him a pair of second, blue eyes to gaze distortedly through. A black caught like this gets to thinking that white people are all right, which isn't hard to believe when he is far enough out of the man's reach and his mother has a civil service job, but then later when he grows up there're other factors to consider. Weird factors which lead to the edge of insanity. He wonders after a while, and he tries again to reorganize his multihued, funny-paper-collage aspected world with strictly white values, thinking white logic with black-white experiences, and often he becomes bitter or skeptical, or worse, especially when he finds it is other blacks closer to him doing him more obvious treachery than the whites.

When he finds that he is not white, even though his mind believes there is a sameness that his inner black eyes cannot detect, he wishes to stop believing in justice, fair play, honor and truth. Why did they prepare me only for this lie? he wonders. When one finds he must become unfeeling out of a sense of protection as those who do not feel nor wish to know or feel, then sometimes he turns his back upon his own people and himself and becomes all the more disillusioned, for that is when he is really alone, and is lost. . . .

The world prepares the black man in a single skill: treachery to his fellows.

No man lies to a black man more than another black man. No man cheats or is as ready to kill another black man as is another black man. One must become accustomed to the perplexities of this brotherhood and learn and understand why. One must lose faith, for faith is never quite enough. One must throw away belief, for belief is held by every black fool. One must be blown apart by all that one has been taught and reassembled in the vacuum of ignorance to form the vessel of new experience.

There is not a white man alone I fear to face, though I am wary of each of my black brothers, for ancient betrayal waits behind each smile and set of dark eyes. All white groups I enter with caution, for the collective will of their numbers is to keep me in *my* place whether it be in front of the firing squad or standing at a podium before an expanse of equally black faces. No black group do I fear alone, but it is the influence of the manipulators in the outer wings which I take care to avoid. It is as true today as it was four hundred years ago in this land: blacks meet together only because some whites desire their congregation, and blacks are compelled to seek fraternity through the urging of white sympathizers and exploiters. The black man is the loneliest human in the universe, and he can sense freedom most when he is unencumbered by the society of his fellow-men who are unwittingly guided by whites.

"Here's a book for you," Len said, handing me a heavy bound book.

The Principles of Marxist Socialism was its title. I handled the gray book with silver lettering; it hadn't been used much and inside the flap was an inscription: "To Lenny, Carol."

"You and your shit," Lou said.

"No, no, no, sister," Connie said. "That's where it's at."

"That's right," Ernest said. "The ends justify the means of the revolution."

There was a quickening in the room and they all began to speak at once of socialism, communism and revolution.

"Man, given my choice I'd rather be a first-class communist den a mahthafukkin' back-ah-de-bus class nigger," Ernest said to someone.

"Books, books," Lou said. "All you chumps do is look in some fukkin' books and talk."

"The wise man goes to the source of knowledge while the fool meets his adversary as the fool," Connie said.

"Tell it like it are, sister," Ernest drawled.

"You see, Steve," Len said, "any method has its limited value; it is the times that make it right and then the people . . ."

"The times are the people," someone cut in.

Len pulled out more books and began questioning me once more about what I had read. I relented. He seemed surprised that I had read so much and could talk to him on most topics he chose, though I didn't know too much about Linus Pauling, the House Un-American Activities Committee or Richard Nixon, except that I despised Nixon.

He began telling me about silk screen prints and from there he went to the finer points of "down home" blues while the radio chanted Gregorian choruses.

The sun sank and dusk crawled into the courtyard like a weary animal. Some of us had been there for twenty-four hours and Len and Lou didn't seem to tire of our company.

A knock sounded on the living room door and Lou hollered out for the visitor to enter. The visitor was a stocky dark fellow. He was a foreigner.

"Hello, Olu," Len greeted the dark man.

"Hello," the man answered. "How is everyone today?"

"Why didn't you come to my party, Olu?" Lou demanded.

"I been very busy."

"Olu," Len said. "I want you to meet a very good friend of ours."

We were introduced and I was told that Olu came from Africa and was a student at a trade school close by. He sat down and refused the wine offered him.

"Have you seen Rick today?" Olu asked. "I'm looking for him."

"No, he left last night after the party and hasn't returned."

"Oh, a very good program is coming on about your homeland," Len told Olu.

"It is?"

"Yes, it will be on soon as this music goes off."

"That's good," Olu said but did not seem especially interested.

Lou began telling Olu how she had made the drapes from burlap Len had bought and made herself a skirt also and a blouse. She asked him when he was going to dress in his African clothes and visit, and then Connie started talking to him in a foreign language that I had not heard before. She wasn't too good, from the way the African had her repeat phrases, but she knew enough for him to answer her rapidly and say something which caused her to laugh. Len told me that Connie and Olu were speaking Swahili.

"How would you folks like some curried rice and yams?" Len asked.

Ernest and I looked at each other and shrugged as Len started for the kitchen, not waiting for any replies. The girls spoke to Olu, Connie in pidgin English and Swahili and Lou edging in a word of English when she could.

"Hey, man, the pluck's all gone," Ernest said to me.

So we decided to walk and get another bottle of wine.

On one of his swings through his old hometown, after he began shipping out, and after his mother had moved across town and his old neighborhood had changed more than he knew, he ran into Dollface, Jess's sister, on Market Street, downtown. She tried to avoid him, he thought because she didn't recognize him and mistook him for somebody getting fresh, for she was grown up now and had turned out to be a stallion, even finer in all quarters than her older sister, Diane. He had stopped her, asked about Jess and gotten their new address. Jess was still living at home with his folks. Walking down the street, after saying good-bye to Dollface, and watching her dynamite body moving across the street, he smiled and knew he would kid Jess about his still being a mamma's boy.

Next day he went to see his old friend. He knocked on the door of the wooden house, and Jess's mother opened it. He introduced himself and kissed her like a son, then she went inside to her son, after talking a little while and saying how much of a man he had grown up to be.

Someone came to the door. He was carrying a child and came out and said, "Stevie Benson . . . as I live and breathe. My . . . you're a sight for sore eyes."

The caller looked at his old friend, who kissed the toddler and put him down to play in the front yard.

"How ya doin', Jess?"

"Just livin', honey . . . just livin'. . . . Where you been keepin' yourself?"

He was high off of something, and his lips were painted with a greasy-looking, almost transparent lipstick, and he puckered his lips grotesquely and grimaced in an exaggerated effeminate way. He

151

wore liberal amounts of the ninety-nine-cent perfume that his friend had smelled once so long ago when he first visited the Simpson family.

"Do you see Homer anymore, Jess?"

"Homer? . . . Homer? . . . Oh, no, chile . . . that ole country nigger punched me one time. I was mindin' my business walkin' down Columbia Avenue with some of my friends, and that bitch just walked up out of nowhere and knocked me on my ass. I heard he's over in Korea . . . in the stupid army. Shit, I hope they start another war and kill his dumb fuckin' ass, baby."

"I'm lookin' for Delores, man. Can you help me locate her?"

"Why, sure, honey . . . just stand up on Broad and Girard any night . . . she's trickin' somewhere around there and hangs out at the Champagne Bowl. But why waste your time on cheap trade like that? . . . I'll take you to a party with me tonight. . . . We still friends, ain't we, Steve?"

"Look, Jess . . . I got to go. My ship's gettin' under way soon. . . . It's been good seein' you, man."

As he turned and began walking away, Jess said:

"The pleasure has been all mine, ole syphy arm Stevie, you ole sweet thing you," and he giggled in his old high and crazy way.

Two years later he was in town again for a while and went to a late night movie alone. When the lights came on between features, someone called him from the back of the theater: "Hey, Chuck. Hey, Chuckie . . . hey, Stevie Benson. Don't make like you don't know me, *fellow.*"

He turned and looked back. It was Jess Simpson. Before he looked back toward the front and ignored Jess, his old friend, now in drag, sporting a blond wig, winked at him.

When the lights went out Stevie Benson snuck out a side door and hailed the first cab that would stop for him. He stopped in a bar near where he was staying and drank steady and played sad records on the jukebox until he was very very drunk.

152

I survived California, america and the great wild and woolly world. At least so far, because I have to go back again one day to my youth and hook up a lot of memories.

Over the years lots of things happened. Len and Lou broke up. Len married a Jewish girl, Sharon, and they broke up after having a son and going through some weird things and are now back together, I hear. I met Lou up in Frisco a couple of years ago. She had married a guy who owned one of those few North Beach bars that remained a bar, even after the topless and bottomless and freak parlors had taken over the neighborhood. He looked Oriental to me, the one time I saw him. Chinatown was around the corner, so I guess the Mafia couldn't muscle him too much. Lou was looking good; had a small baby and was really happy in appearance.

Rick and Tanya got married. His fortunes fell after rising greatly during the Black Revolution period, when he was a large Cultural Nationalist figure, and Tanya fell out with him publicly when he seems to have tripped out.

Lots of things have changed over the years. I could really write a book about it all, if I had the discipline or was hungry enough. I've met and worked with most of the young names in the black movement at one time or another, in the limited capacity that I can serve them—black communications is my interest—and I have tried to keep my sense of humor and my capacity to learn and change with the times.

That's what it's all about, isn't it? Change. Well, if you want to know somebody who has gone through changes, look no farther. It's been a very eventful decade. But I don't talk about it all, if you know what I mean.

He kicked the television cord outta the outlet, dousing the remaining light in her white-walled apartment, but for the shine of the full moon and those unexpected autos whose lights swing across the ceiling as they crest the hill at the seat of the window. Stop! What are you doing? He smashed her aside her blond head, the stringy hair catching the moon, her gray face a void, the mouth opening. Flash of pearly teeth. Smash. Quiet! Undress. Please don't. Do you want me to choke you to unconsciousness and then take it? Don't tear my clothes off. There. Oh, don't. The broad flat pimpled white behind held in the palms of his hands, the black fingers and thumb digging in. Push push. You're hurting me. Don't. Ummmm . . . hardly any smell. Scratch of blond hairs. In the bed, in the bed. Not here on the floor, please. Not like a dog. You hurt. Shut up. But I think I'm bleeding. Moon. Night. Again. Can I get something to drink? I won't cry, I won't cry. The flesh. Pale, jewish, european. She'll never learn to screw with her stiff ass. Stiff hard black meat in her. And the hurting palm/hand. I won't scream. No noise. Not again, please. Again. No, I don't want any. It's not about what you want. But it isn't pleasant to me. I hate you. I hate you. I hate you. Slam! Yes, I'll be quiet. Don't hurt. I'll keep quiet. Again. No, don't. the slime. the slow greasy ooze of white stuff. Can I go to the bathroom? oh, don't watch. I won't scream. you bit me. God, if I get a baby or breast cancer . . . please, not again. I'm tired and sore. Let's just lay here together.

Sun. Clang of trolleys. Memories of before sleep and awakening. Look to see if alive. Damn, this nigger was born lucky. She coulda called the cops, she coulda . . . he feels his balls, joint/self. smell of

154

bacon/coffee/eggs. . . . her female hum behind the door. her. kitchen door swings out. herself. Plugs in TV. another white face. Morning. How you snore, man. tray set down. a morning kiss of pink lips on his kinky black head. What's her name? white, american face, brown eyes and a hope of a freckle, blond midwestern hair. the puny breasts behind the magic Maidenform   the flat white ass with the brown hairs   the tight hygienic pussy that never closes. gotta run, baby. work, you know. you gave me *two* black eyes, jeezus. i'll have to wear my shades and have the kids at the office kiddin' me about being kooky or something. do you know my name yet? here's my extra key. I'll see you tonight, won't I, honey? there's some money in the night table drawer in case you want to go somewhere before I get back. but i'll see you tonight, huh? We have a lot to catch up on. this is gonna be a groovy day. . . . *i hurt all over.* . . .

A white guy killed a lot of people one day in Camden, N.J., just across the river from us. We were standing on the corner that night. I was the youngest and newest member of the Snakes.

"Hey, ya hear 'bout that mahthafukker killin' all them people over in Camden today?" Coozie asked.

"Yeah . . . the mahthafukker did in twelve crackers," said Reddie.

"Thirteen," I chimed in.

"Twelve," Reddie repeated.

"Thirteen," I replied.

Reddie looked at me, dropped his head and put his hands on his hips.

Being young and unwise, I rolled my eyes and pouted, having my hands in both my pockets, my classic stance at that time.

Reddie smashed me in the mouth, almost knocking me out. I put

155

up my hands and fought a one-sided boxing match with one of the best street fighters I've ever known.

When it was over and the Snakes were patching me up and getting me drunk so I wouldn't be "feelin' no pain," after Reddie had shaken my hand and said that I had a lot of heart for a youngblood but wouldn't live to tell the story if I didn't learn to understand who I was, where I was at and under what conditions I was allowed, I promised myself to keep my mouth shut and my eyes open.

And I also broke the habit of standing around in the streets with my hands in my pockets.

She licked her pink, violet-veined tongue over her large pouting lips and said, "Tell me a dirty story . . . sweetdaddy . . . so I can get even mo' hotter fo you."

And I thought a moment, held her black behind tighter, inserted my forefinger inside her vagina, tried to locate the clitoris and replied, "Yeah, baby . . . okay . . . okay . . . I'll tell you one of my L.A. stories."

Once in L.A. I had this roommate . . . yeah, he had vanilla fever . . . you know, he loved himself some white girls. And we shared this tiny tiny pad just off of Santa Monica . . . not yet Hollywood, quite . . . a sleeping place, really, with only a bath, a room large enough for a let/down wall bed and couch and a chair, a tiny kitchen and two closets. I slept in one. Yeah, one of the closets. Really! It was this kinda big walk/in closet and I slept in it on this small fold/up bed, behind a dingy curtain, with my feet stuck/out beneath, into the living room. . . . That's how anybody who came to visit knew I was in, if I was sleepin' . . . 'cause they could see my feet soon as the door swung open, and even before they heard me snoring.

Now one night while I was stretched out on my little bed, Ernie, that was my roomie's name, Ernest, brought this jewish broad to our pad. He had been fuckin' this bitch for a while. Her name was Cherry. And they were comin' on strong together. Cherry acted like she was going to move Ernie's other skunks out. He had about six other skanky little jew bitches that he would run into our place, but that was mostly during the day between classes at the school we was goin' to, City College, and I didn't mind if I had to take a walk at noon. I could make it to the library, ya know. Or go down to the bookstore where I worked and browse or hang out or check out a sister. Yeah . . . I was deep into sisters . . . have always been. And Ernie knew I didn't appreciate him too much bringin' all those funky white girls around, but that was his thing.

So they came in that night drunk as two skunks. Couldn't explain to Ernie that this was too much! Morning, noon and now midnight, a line of California jew girls beating a path to our door. To see him! What if my Black Nationalist friends found out my living situation?

Well, I was layin' back on my little bed. I had a lamp rigged back there and I was reading—musta been *Pimp*—when I heard the key in the door, Cherry's giggles and Ernie's "Be cool, baby." And then the door closed and remarks by Cherry about my feet being white on the bottom. And then the sound of the wall bed swinging down. By then I knew it was time to get up. Which I did.

"Hey, man . . . what's happenin'?" Ernie said to me as I squeezed from around my bed, shoved the curtain aside and stumbled into the room, stuffing my shirt into my pants and carrying my sandals.

"Nothin', man . . . nothin'," I said.

"Your fly's open, baby," Cherry said to me, her large silver-looped earrings and bracelets chattering. And I found the bathroom, shut the door and got myself together.

Back in the living room the radio was playing the Chambers Brothers and Ernie was pouring Red Mountain burgundy into Cherry's cup that she now kept in our kitchen, a large pink cup with two crimson cherries painted on the sides.

"Want some wine, man?" Ernie asked.

"Nawh, I'm takin' a walk."

"Thanks," Cherry said.

"Don't mention it." And I left.

Now I had a tremendous hard-on for Cherry, which may seem contradictory, seeing that I had leanings toward neophyte Black Nationalism back then, and later for Black Revolution, but that night I could hardly get Cherry's pale image out of my brain. I tried not to admit this to myself, but I did really have it for that devil lady. And it wasn't so much giving up the pad at midnight to Ernie that ranked me, those kinds of emergencies happen; and he would have done the same for me, I knew, as he did do sometime later when I finally made it with Mona, but that night I was thinking of Cherry's sexy flat behind, and her small pouting tits, and her horsy angular face with its strong nose commanding the center like a phallic piece of gristle.

There's not always places to go at midnight, even in large cities. Someone once told me that cities like Philly and Baltimore have the aspects of being large cities, but with almost none of the advantages . . . though if you knew where to go, well, you were there. At least that was the drift of their suggestion. But I knew where I was going that night in L.A. The Xanadu Coffeehouse and Astrological Health Food Snack Bar.

When I got inside, after a fifteen-minute walk up the block from my apartment house, across Vermont Avenue, then cutting around the buildings of the L.A.C.C. campus, then through the parking lots, passing the tennis court, and walking along Monroe briefly, the night was found inside waiting for me. Slinky-type night people were draped across the candle/lit tables, conversing about deep deep subjects: "What's your sign?" "Have you checked out STP?" "Etc." Freaked/out little acid hippies nodded or were zunked/out upon pillows and couches. Hell's Angels laid dead, waiting to stomp *anyone,* but finding little target material in that atmosphere of coffeehouse/folk-music-on-the-weekends-off-campus-Bohemia.

I ordered an avocado and watercress sandwich on nut bread and a glass of guava juice. Cherry was on my mind. Cherry. That very moment, I knew, Ernie was sockin' it to her and the vision of their drunken pawing made my joint as stiff as a pickle.

"What's on your mind, baby?" Toni said to me as she slid upon the stool next to me. She was a friend's woman, wife of an Anglo/Mexican painter of the abstract nudes of his memory, Toni of the pointed tits and overly made-up face, her brunette hair draped down over one eye like a somebody famous in the movies. I swung toward her on my stool so she could see my hard pants front and looked into her green eyes.

"How's the sandwich?" she asked.

"Great."

I offered; she took a bite.

"Hey . . . what's on your mind?" she said, chewing. "Does she have a name?"

I was almost through with the sandwich.

"Where's Perez?" I asked.

"Painting."

"Ain't he ever goin'a use you anymore?"

"He says the bodies within his absurd imagination are more perfect for his purposes than I could ever be," she said.

"Wow . . . Let's go get a drink."

"Okay."

Down the street in the bar the jukebox was playing country and western. I was the only black in sight. It was payday for me.

"How 'bout wine?" I asked.

"You're buyin'."

The place was nearly empty and the roller derby was on TV, turned down low.

"You still with that faggot?"

She looked hurt.

"I thought you wanted to drink," she said.

"Guess I'm in a lousy mood."

I leaned over and kissed her on the cheek. The Texas/style bartender looked us over but hid his scowl.

"Maybe we should go," she said.

"Let's just drink. I'm as lonely as you are."

She sighed. Her breasts heaved under the light blouse to show her nipples plainly.

"All he does is paint. Paint!"

"Yeah . . . I know," I said.

"Doesn't even try to sell it. Just spreads paint on those big goddamn boards."

We got served and drank fast and talked about her problems.

"You still write poetry?" she asked.

"I guess."

"I've got the car . . . let's take a ride."

She had a Studebaker that was tied together by wire and hope. We put seventy-five cents' worth of gas in it, picked up a bottle of port and drove up above the Sunset Strip, drinking all the way and listening to soul music on the tinny AM radio.

"Let's get in the back seat," she said after we had found a dark and private place.

In the back I slipped off her shorts and for ten minutes we strained and humped. I felt her shudder and I could hold myself no longer.

It was the first time we had made it together. I didn't like her too much. Her box was too big to suit me.

"I like you," she said.

"You do?"

"I guess I'm lonely."

"We both are," I replied. She drank long from the bottle. I did likewise.

Then she slipped from the seat and placed her head between my legs.

"I love to do this," she said, taking her first breath since going down. "You don't mind, do you?"

"Nawh," I sighed.

160

She sucked and I drank more of the wine, while running my hand through her bobbing stringy hair. I thought of Cherry and what she was doing then to Ernie. And suddenly, Toni's serpentine tongue crawled into a place inside me, within my inner skull, behind my panicky eyes, like her pink muscle was inside my brain scooping out the gray meat clinging to the roof of my head, and I screamed silently, nearly fainting, feeling as if I were about to wet myself or fart; and she sucked loudly, until all of me was spilling into her gluttonous mouth as I weakly held myself back, held my jerking down to the level of a paralyzed quiver to keep my clawing hands from snatching her greedy head away from the head of my penis.

It was over.

"I loved that," she said, wiping her lips on her forearm. "Is there any more wine?"

I took my last drink and gave the bottle to her to kill.

"Do you want any more?" she said as she fondled my limp joint.

"Maybe later."

My clothes were on straight and I was telling her of my ambitions when I heard them. She started to an erect position, bumping her head on the roof of the small car, then fell back and snatched up her crumpled shorts to hide her pubic hairs as the flashlight beam poked into the window.

"L.A.P.D.," the voice said. "You there . . . step out, please."

I knew the voice meant me. As I got out on the side of the light I glanced back and saw Toni's nipples blushing in the light beam. Someone opened the door on her side and got in.

"Can I see your license and registration, please," the policeman said.

I showed him what I had.

"This isn't your car?"

"It belongs to my friend inside," I said. "The registration is on the sun visor."

Soft talk came from within the car and the radio still played.

"Walk over to my car with me," the cop said to me. "I have to make a report."

In back of some trees waited the police car. He stretched me over the hood and felt me for guns, knives, drugs and kicks.

"Where's your marijuana?" he said.

"There ain't any," I replied.

"Knock off the bullshit. You better tell me now where it's at," he said. "When I take you downtown it'll go easier on you."

He pretended to call up the station house and then hassled me for ten more minutes until his partner came back alone.

"She's pretty clever," his partner said to him. "You better go back and check out her story. I'll keep our friend Shine here company."

The first cop stole into the darkness.

"Want a cigarette?" the new cop asked.

"Nawh . . . don't smoke."

"You're lucky," he said.

We talked about colleges. He had gone to Valley State. The draft. He'd been in the Marines.

After a while the first one was back.

"She's not bad," he said to his partner.

"You know you could get into a lot of trouble, Sambo, don't you?" the other one said to me.

I nodded.

"You better head back," one of them said to me before they climbed into their car, turned on their parking lights and crept from the trees and down the trail.

"Was it bad?" I said to her when I got back to the car.

She held me and kissed me on my neck.

"No . . . not at all. Pigs don't bother me."

We drove back to the coffeehouse in silence. The few remaining Angels were mounting their metal beasts and varooming off in the direction of the ocean. Several teenyboppers that Toni knew were standing at the curb. We opened the door and they climbed in the back. One turned us on to some Panama Red. It really fucked me up.

"There's a party in Venice," someone said.

I told them I couldn't make that.

"Thanks for helping me," Toni said as I got out.

"Helping you?"

"Yeah . . . with my loneliness."

"Sure."

The bar I stopped at on my way home was empty. I drank red wine, not the sweet kind, until I was drunk.

When my key unlocked my apartment door the night chain stopped me, and I heard heavy snoring from within the space.

"They're sleepin'," I said drunkenly to myself.

Then I called out about a dozen times and knocked and really knew they were asleep.

"I'm gonna wake the whole goddamn place up," I mumbled aloud before I realized that I should shut up.

Finally, I put my hand and forearm through the door opening and tried to unfasten the chain. No good. I wasn't going to get anywhere that way. So I took out my switchblade and pushed my hand and arm through the hole and around the doorjamb.

It must have been an hour later when the last screw fell from the inside fixture and I gave the door a short jerk, and was inside. The snoring continued. The light thrown by the door's brief opening showed me Ernie and Cherry sleeping in each other's arms, Cherry's ivory leg slinking from beneath the sheet.

With the door closed silently behind me, I dropped to my knees and listened. They still snored. Then I crawled to the side of the bed, and waited. Cherry shifted some and her leg fell from the side of the bed, grazing my shoulder, and hung there. I waited and listened. Then I took my right hand and felt up her leg until I found her pussy, then I began fingering the places that I knew would arouse her. Her breathing rhythm changed. I took my hand away. And I heard Cherry turn over, her bracelets making tinny jangles in the silence, and shift upon the bed before slurping sounds began.

I didn't think I should look up over the side of the bed then because a pale light showed around the edges of the drawn shades and shapes in that room were distinguishable in the moonlight.

The bed creaked and I slid under it. Then the bed began pounding, the metal springs, between me and the mattress, upon my back, rising and falling diabolically.

Squeak squonk squeak squonk squeak squonk . . . the bed made that sound as it rose and fell upon my back and backside, my hands folded over and protecting the back of my head and neck. There was loud breathing and moans and sighs up topside on the bed where Cherry had somehow mounted Ernie after getting or having his dick hard enough for her to ride it viciously, like a witch must stay astride her broom, as I learned when I crawled away from under the punishment of the torture rack of that mattress and spring beating me to a crushed hamburger; for I looked back and saw Cherry in the dim light, white as a devil, upon my roommate, Ernest, fucking him unconscious, for he had not awakened from his stupor, only was being ravished—*completely*—his instrument of pleasure, his black naked self, his very memory of that dark, sexual dawn.

A violent convulsion struck Cherry on one of her mighty downward swoops and she gagged and expelled gasps of strangled breath from her constricted throat; her sputum sprayed coughing upon my head as I tried to duck away from the frenzy of that last moment of their coupling.

After a while the sleep rhythms returned to their breathing and bed postures, and I crept out the door and closed it, then went downstairs and sat in the lobby reading *Saturday Evening Post*s and *Look*s until the mailman came, the sun being up by then.

Later, I pushed upon my door again. It gave. Ernie was partially dressed, shoving the wall bed back in place.

"Hey, man . . . How you doin'?" he asked.

"Okay . . . I guess," I replied.

"Sorry if we inconvenienced you, my man."

"That's okay," I said. "I came in anyway. . . . While you were sleepin'. Took the night chain off from the outside. . . . Didn't stay."

"Oh, yeah . . . Well, me and Cherry's hattin' up, ain't we, mama?"

164

Cherry came out of the bathroom, a towel around her.

"Yeah, baby . . . anything you say, Ernie," she said to him.

"I'm just picking up some books," I said. "Got an early class . . . but when I get home I would like to get some sleep."

"No problem," Ernie assured. "Me and Cherry's goin'a Frisco for a couple of days. . . . You got it, brother."

"Okay, see you, Ernie," I said after getting my books. "See you, Cherry."

Cherry, her back to Ernie, winked at me and adjusted her bracelets. The things made the room sound like a metal factory.

"Bye . . . yawhl," she said with a smile.

"And I left," I told the luscious black shape beside me.

"You did?"

"Yeah . . . and three days later I found out that I had the claps."

"Ohhh . . . You took care of that, didn't you, honey?" she asked.

"Sure . . . that was a long time ago."

My finger slipped out.

"Wait a minute, honey. . . . Do my clit-tor-*rus.*"

"Okay . . . baby . . . okay," I said.

She moved my hand away and placed her own finger between her legs. In a second I felt her tremble.

"Ahhh . . . if you only knew where my clit-tor-*rus* was, baby . . . like I do."

"It's cli-to-ris."

"What?"

"Cli-to-ris!"

"Oh, really? . . . I guess that's why I like you so much, Stevie . . . you're an intellectual."

"Awww . . . not really," I said bashfully.

"Sure you are, baby. . . . You're not at all like a lot of those other freaks I know," she answered.

She snuggled close up under me and wrapped her big dark legs around me.

"Uummm . . . I really got a good nut, daddy. Don't you want to fuck me now?" She sighed in my ear and stuck her tongue almost into my brain. "I'll let you com' in mah mouf."

We rolled over.

"You really tell some good dirty stories, baby," she said as I pushed my thing in her and fell into limbo. "But they ain't nasty enough . . . and they so weird."

"Ouch, sweetdaddy!" she cried, when I definitely began stroking . . . and the shit was on.

> Mah poppa's a jockey an he teach me how ta ride . . . oh, yeah, mah poppa's a jockey an he teach me how ta ride . . . he said git in da middle son an' ya move from side to side . . .

166